SUGAR AND SPICE, INK

EVAN GRACE

Definition of Stencil:

Template of a tattoo that is applied to the skin so the tattooist has a basic outline.

SIERRA

I run to the bathroom just as the contents of my stomach come out. Thankfully I didn't miss the toilet this time because that was not pretty. After I flush the toilet, I get up and brush my teeth. Back in my bedroom I crawl onto my bed and curl into a protective ball.

I can't shake this stomach bug, and I've been sick for over a week now. Yes, I know one might think I am pregnant, but I took a test, and it was negative. Of course, it could've been too early or a false negative. Oh fuck, who am I kidding; I'm so pregnant.

Between my late period, the puking, and my tender breasts, how could I deny something that is clearly setting off red alerts loud and clear.

I blow out a breath and grab my cell phone. I scroll through my contacts and find Dr. Honn, my OB/Gyn's number, and press the call button. When the receptionist answers, I give her my name and explain that I need to come in for an appointment.

I'm lucky, and they can see me on Thursday, so I only have to wait two days. I don't remember my older sister Mona having morning sickness when she was pregnant with my niece, but everyone is different.

I climb off the bed and stand in front of my full-length mirror. I grab the hem of my tank top and pull it up, turning to the side. My stomach is still flat for now, but do my boobs look bigger?

I cup them and give them a little squeeze. They don't feel bigger.

In the living room, I curl up on the sofa and turn on the TV. I watch Keeping Up with the Kardashians and can't help but wonder what I'm going to say to Nick. Well, I'm not saying anything until I get confirmation from the doctor.

More than likely he's going to run when I tell him I'm pregnant anyway. Our arrangement was just sex, wasn't it? It hasn't felt like just sex since our first weekend together.

I've tried to break things off multiple times, but either he ignores me or I come back because I can't get enough of him, and I miss him. It's like I've finally met my other half. When we're together it's effortless. He scares me to death. I always thought something was wrong with me because of my high sex drive, but I just love sex; better yet, I love sex with Nick.

Ugh, I feel like shit, and I'm still getting horny just thinking about him, but I'm not calling him until I know for sure what's going on.

"Well, Sierra, you're definitely pregnant, and about six weeks along." Dr. Honn smiles as she delivers the news. "You're due date is August sixteenth." She hands me a piece of paper. "This is a prescription for prenatal vitamins."

She goes over tips for the morning sickness and tells me she wants me to make an appointment for four weeks, and we'll try to hear the heartbeat then.

"Do you have any questions?" I shake my head because right now I can't think.

Dr. Honn walks me to the reception desk and congratulates me before disappearing in the back. Outside, I pull out my phone and dial Nick.

"Hey, sexy, what are you up to?" His voice alone makes me do a full body shiver.

I take a deep breath. "I need to see you. We have to talk."

He sighs into the phone. "Here we go again. If you're about to break things off with me again then no, I don't want to talk." Nick disconnects, and I stare down at my phone in shock.

My stomach turns because of course he thinks I'm about to break things off. I've done it since we met. I've never connected to someone the way I've connected with him. Yes, he's gorgeous, but he's loud, he says inappropriate things all of the time, and he's always surrounded by beautiful women ever since he became the co-owner of Atlanta's arena football team. We've connected on a sexual level, but it's so much more than that.

When I was in college, I swore I'd found the love of my life, and things were great with Lance until they weren't. I'd been home for a visit and had decided to head back to school to surprise him at his apartment. That was when I found him plowing his best friend, Ben.

I was heartbroken and devastated because our whole relationship was one big fucking lie. I was his beard and didn't even know it; well, obviously I didn't.

After that I kept it to casual fucks and one-night stands until I met Nick. We met while my sisters and I took Iris, my niece, on a little weekend getaway before school started back up.

The moment that giant man walked up to me, ignoring everyone else, I felt like I'd had a tiny orgasm. We ditched everyone. First, we went to the resort bar and had a couple of drinks. It didn't take long before we made our way toward his room.

We barely made it inside before he had me against the wall. I'd been with quite a few men, I wasn't going to apologize, or be embarrassed, but I'd never been with a man with a cock as large as Nick's. With as big as he is, I would've been disappointed had it not been proportionate with the rest of him.

It was long with the most perfect girth. We fit together perfectly. In one night we'd had sex against the wall, on his bed, and outside while snuggling in front of the fire pit.

By the time the weekend was over, I felt like I was walking bow-legged and was certain I'd never hear from him again.

That didn't happen, of course, and ever since

we've had this on and off again relationship. I've ended things multiple times, mainly when things were getting too relationship-y.

I hate it and feel bad every time, but I swore I was never going to allow myself to get hurt again. That man has the power to destroy me, whether he knows it or not.

I pull up his contact information again, but it goes straight to voicemail. "Nick, please call me back. It's not what you think, but I need to talk to you. Please come over tonight, or I can come to you. Please." I don't want to beg, but I also need to talk to him.

Back at my apartment I park in my designated parking spot. I climb out of my car and head into my building. It's not the fanciest apartment, but it's clean, safe, and the manager is a good guy who will actually fix stuff if it's broken.

I let myself in as my stomach begins to growl. I ignore it and try calling Nick again, but it goes right to voicemail. "Hey, it's me. I didn't want to leave this on your voicemail, but since you're not taking my calls I have no choice." Fuck, I can't do this over voicemail. "Please just call me back or come over." I lower my voice to almost a whisper. "I really need to talk to you ... please."

After making myself a bowl of chicken noodle soup, I eat it while standing on my balcony watching for him, but by the time I finish my soup I accept the fact that he's not coming.

I put my bowl in the sink and head back to my bedroom to get ready to head to the studio. Lucky for me, my morning sickness is strictly morning, mostly, so I'm able to make it through the workday.

I haven't told my brother, sisters, or parents yet; not that I don't want to, but I want Nick to know first. Plus Mona and her man Joaquin are settling in to cohabitative bliss, and I didn't want to disrupt it.

They waited until right after New Year's to make the move, which was really easy since Iris already had her own room there, and they both had clothes there.

In my bedroom I throw on a pair of holey jeans, my black Sugar and Spice, Ink V-neck t-shirt, and black Nikes. I do my makeup, curl my platinum blonde locks, and then spray them with hair spray.

I grab the box of saltines and dump a couple of cans of ginger ale into my Yeti cup. My phone taunts me, and I pick it up—no call from Nick yet. Disappointment fills me as I shove it in my bag along with the box of saltines. I'm starving, but I know better than to try to eat before I do some ink.

Last week I'd eaten a chicken sandwich before I went in, and halfway through the sleeve I was working on the food came right back up. That was the first sign that something wasn't right. Anyway, luckily after I got rid of the sandwich I was good to go.

Thirty minutes later I pull into the parking lot of Sugar and Spice, Ink. I'm so proud of the work we've done here. We've made a name for ourselves in the tattoo industry. One that we worked damn hard for.

Inside I find my sister Greta at the counter with our new apprentice, Lainey, sitting with her and learning how to make appointments, downloading designs for upcoming appointments, as well as the paperwork clients will fill out when they come in.

"Hey, ladies." I kiss Greta's cheek as I walk by and head toward the office. My beautiful sister Mona sits behind the desk typing on the computer. "Hey, you. I didn't see your car out there."

She smiles up at me. "Joaquin dropped me off. He and the kids were running to the store to get stuff for me to make cupcakes for Iris and Max's class."

Joaquin insisted that Iris go to the same school as his son and insisted that he pay for it. That was one of the worst fights they've had, but Joaquin just wanted Iris to have the same advantages as Max because he loves our girl. She finally relented when she saw how important it was and then how excited Max was about the possibility of Iris going to school with him.

I know Mona was worried about Iris fitting in. My niece is certainly a free spirit, but that's what we love about our girl. Joaquin swore that Max would make the transition smooth for her, and so far he has.

I set my bag on the loveseat across from the desk. My stomach does a little pitch, and I take a sip of my ginger ale.

"Are you okay? You look a little green." Mona gets up and comes toward me.

I take another sip of my drink. "I'm fine. I think I have a touch of that stomach bug going around. I'll wear a mask while I work."

Joaquin and the kids show up to get Mona, and my other sisters and I go outside to say hi to everyone. That sweet little Max is already calling us aunt and gives us high fives because he's too cool for hugs. They take off after I get hugs and smoochies from Iris. We head inside, and I wait for my appointment to show up.

I wipe off my station as my last appointment pays Greta, whom thankfully stuck around to walk out with me. In between clients I kept checking my phone, but I haven't heard anything from Nick. He's probably out banging as many women as he can; no, I'm not going to get all negative.

Greta comes into the back and hands me some cash. "She tipped you a hundred dollars." I take it from her and stuff it into my back pocket.

"She's so sweet and generous. She always over tips when she comes in." After I shut down my station, I head into the office and put my money in my bag then pop a peppermint into my mouth.

"What was with the mask tonight?" My sister steps inside the office.

I smile at her and shrug. "I just wasn't feeling that great and thought I'd better be cautious." I look my younger sister, and our resident piercer, over. "You look so pretty today." Most of her body is covered in beautiful ink that Mona, Heidi, and myself have worked on. Her long brown hair hangs down her back in beautiful waves.

She's the tallest of us girls and has a body that any woman would kill for; feminine but lean and the perfect hourglass. Her piercings which include small gauges in each ear, a piercing in each cheek, septum, nipples, belly button, and clitoral hood, are amazing. Well, okay, I don't know about her nether region piercing or her nipples, but the others are so feminine on her.

17

Greta's been featured in tattoo and piercing magazines and is quickly becoming an influencer on Instagram.

She blushes and tucks her hair behind her ear. "Thanks. I tried this new makeup line. It's vegan and so light I don't feel like I'm wearing anything. Are you about ready?"

"Yep." I follow her out after setting the alarm. We paid a lot of money for the security system we have, but some of our equipment is expensive.

I'm sure she's heading back to the apartment she shares with our baby sister Heidi. When I reach mine I find Nick's new red Mercedes AMG GT in the guest parking spot next to mine. It's such a douchy car, but he does look sexy when he drives it.

As soon as I climb out of my car, he climbs out of his. Damn, he makes my stomach flutter every time I look at him. His dark blond hair is styled to look messy, but you know he totally styled it. Nick's blue eyes are framed by thick, dark lashes.

He meets me on the sidewalk. "I didn't expect to see you," I say quietly as I walk with him toward the doors. Nick hasn't made a move to touch me, and it's got me freaking out because normally he can't keep his hands off of me.

I feel Nick at my back as we walk up the stairs. He's angry, and I can feel it coming off of him in waves. "I wasn't going to come because I know what's about to happen, but let's hurry and get this over with." I let us into my apartment and tell him to have a seat. My heart begins to pound in my chest, my stomach is doing so many flips, and my hands tremble.

I sit on my coffee table right in front of him so we're facing each other. It's probably best to just say it and get it out. I open my mouth to speak, but he holds his hand up.

"Before you say whatever it is you're going to say, I want to say something. You've done nothing but lead me around by my dick since the beginning. I'll admit I was a willing participant, but that's done. You're not going to jerk me around anymore, breaking things off one minute and then come climbing on my cock the next. We're done."

My eyes begin to burn, and I'm about to throw up what little I ate. "You need to leave." I'm proud of myself for sounding so strong at the moment.

He stands and walks to the door, turning to me as he raises his brow. "What were you going to tell me? Not like I don't already know what it is."

I open the door for him to walk through, and he steps onto the porch then turns back to me. I look into his eyes and announce, "I'm pregnant," right before I slam the door in his face.

SIERRA

It takes a good five minutes before Nick starts pounding on my door, but I'm not going to answer it—not right now. I know our weird relationship was just sex, or it was supposed to be, but this hurts ... bad.

"Sierra, open the door."

I swipe roughly at the tears that run down my cheeks with the back of his hand. "Go home, Nick. I don't want to talk right now." My voice catches at the end. I look through the peephole to find him pacing back and forth in front of the door.

"Please, Sierra, let me in. Let's talk about this, okay?"

I clear my throat and stand my ground. "N-not tonight, Nick. I'm tired, and I want to go to bed."

Moments tick by as Nick paces the porch, remaining quiet. He slows his strides and leans against the door, bracing both hands on the frame.

"I'll give you tonight, Sierra, but promise we'll talk tomorrow." I don't miss the desperate look on his face.

"I promise, Nick." He doesn't move right away, but after a few minutes he pushes off the door and rubs his hands through his hair. As soon as he's gone, I grab my phone and send a text to Mona.

Sierra: Are u up?

The dots bounce almost immediately.

Mona: Of course. What's up?

Sierra: Can I come stay with you guys tonight?

Mona: Yes, come over. Are you okay?

My sister is my best friend in the whole wide world. She's definitely my ride or die girl.

Sierra: I'm fine. I just don't want to be alone tonight.

I quickly pack a bag to take with me and lock up my place. This time of night traffic's not bad, so I'm able to get to their fancy ass home in twenty minutes. As soon as I pull in the driveway my sister is standing in the open doorway.

I grab my bag and then walk directly into my sister's arms. "Is it Nick?" she asks quietly. That's what sucks about this whole thing—Nick and Joaquin are best friends, and I don't want to put Mona or Joaquin in the middle.

"Kind of," I say, because I'm not ready to tell Mona about the pregnancy. She'd never judge, but until I get things with him sorted out I want to keep this to myself.

"We don't have to talk, but let's drown ourselves in cupcakes. I have lots of extras." Of course she does because she spoils her man and her kids, and that's okay because I've never seen my sister happier than she is right now.

At the breakfast bar she sets a cupcake with lavender frosting and rainbow sprinkles on top in front of me.

"Do you want wine or milk?"

I'd love a huge glass of wine, but obviously I have to choose the milk. She sets a glass in front of me and then takes the seat next to mine. "Where's Joaq?"

"He's sitting outside drinking a beer. He was giving us privacy if we needed it." See, the guy is amazing.

We eat our cupcakes in silence, partly because it's so delicious and also because I just don't even know what to say. I finish my cupcake and grab our wrappers to throw them away. "Nick broke things off with me," I say when I return to the breakfast bar, taking my seat.

"What? Really? Did he say why?"

"He said he's tired of me leading him around by his dick." I rest my head in my hand, leaning on the counter.

Mona grabs my hand. "I'm not taking his side, but do you think that maybe that's what you've been doing?"

I shrug. "Maybe. We were supposed to just be having sex. Things weren't supposed to become serious." I open my mouth to tell her I'm pregnant, but change my mind at the last second. I reach out grabbing a loose strand of her hair. "I love this color." It's gray with a hint of lavender.

"Thanks. I'm glad I decided to do it. I almost did baby blue, but she showed me this one, and I had to do it."

Joaquin comes inside, greeting me with a side hug before kissing my sister. I won't lie, I'm a little jealous of what they have. The love he feels for Mona and my niece is all I could ever hope for. "The room down from the kids' is all ready for you."

"Thank you. Sorry to disrupt your night." I smile up at him.

"It's seriously no trouble. The kids will be happy to see you in the morning." He looks at Mona. "I've got a couple of things to do in my office." Joaquin kisses her again before leaving the room.

Mona watches him walking out of the room, and I swear she's got hearts swirling around her head. "I'm so happy for you and Iris."

She grabs my hand between both of hers. "How are you, really? Because you look hella sad right now."

"I'm hurt, mad, and embarrassed. I don't know what I'm going to do, Mo." I yawn because I'm honestly so exhausted. I'm not sure if it's the baby, but I need to sleep, and I need to avoid letting Mona answer.

We stand, and I insist that she doesn't need to walk me upstairs. I hug her and make my way up to the spare bedroom. I change into a black tank top and a pair of boxers I stole from Nick.

In the bathroom I quickly wash my face and moisturize. I brush my hair out and throw it into a knot on top of my head and then brush my teeth.

Once I crawl into bed I place my hand on my

lower stomach, still amazed that there is a baby in there. "If it ends up just being you and me, I'm going to love you so much you're not going to know any different."

I roll over to my side, close my eyes, and drift off to sleep.

I open my eyes and blink as my eyes adjust to my surroundings. "Where am I?" It takes a second for the cobwebs to clear. I realize I'm at Mona and Joaquin's, and then I remember why. I'm going to have to talk to Nick today. My stomach turns at the thought because, honestly, I don't know what I'm going to say.

I sit up and take some slow, deep breaths, praying I don't get sick. After a couple of minutes I stand, and my stomach stays sort of calm, so I grab my stuff and hop into the shower.

Once I'm done, I throw on a long-sleeved Sugar and Spice, Ink hoodie the color of raspberries, over the tank top. I brush my hair out and then throw it back up in a bun. I head downstairs and smile when I find my niece and nephew sitting at the bar eating breakfast.

My sister and her man are drinking coffee while leaning against the counter. "Good morning."

Iris smiles at me. "Auntie Sierra! I didn't know you were here for a sleepover." I walk around and kiss the top of her head.

"Hey, Maximum." I ruffle his hair and give him a side hug.

He smiles at me. "Hey, Auntie Sierra."

"Good morning, guys." I look at Mona and Joaquin's coffee lovingly, but I can't have any, and that makes me sad. "Do you have any juice?"

Joaquin grabs the orange juice and pours me a glass. I thank him and take a big sip. I snag a piece of toast from Iris' plate and take a bite. As soon as I swallow it down my stomach turns.

"Sierra?" Mona stares at me. "Are you okay? You look a little green."

I run into the bathroom in the hall and throw up the bite of toast and orange juice. Nasty. I feel a hand rub my back and know it's my sister.

"You don't have a stomach bug; you're pregnant." There's no judgment in her tone, just concern. "Does Nick know?"

I nod and rest my cheek on the seat. I begin to tell her about the phone call and how he assumed I was breaking things off again and what transpired afterward. In the distance I hear pounding and then male voices.

I close my eyes and take a deep breath. When I open my eyes, I find my baby daddy standing in the doorway and proceed to throw up … again.

NICK

I've got a headache to end all headaches when I climb out of bed. When I went home I couldn't stop thinking about the look on Sierra's face when I told her I was breaking things off. Then she kicked me out, and while slamming the door in my face she gave me the most shocking news.

I'm going to be a dad. I've never thought about having kids. Kids never factored into any of my plans. The moment those words slipped from Sierra's lips all I could picture was a little girl with blonde hair and blue eyes like her mama, and it didn't freak me out one bit.

Instead, my big motherfucking mouth got me into trouble—it isn't the first time it's caused me problems. Now I hope she talks to me and will forgive me for being stupid.

I take a quick shower and throw on a pair of gray Brunello Cucinelli wool dress pants and a black

Tom Ford classic barrel cuff dress shirt.

I put on my belt and stick my wallet into my back pocket. After putting on some of the cologne that Sierra loves, I slip on a pair of black Ferragamo's. I climb into my ride and head toward Sierra's.

When I pull into the parking lot I find her spot empty. Pulling out my phone, I send a quick text to Joaquin.

Nick: Hey, man, is Sierra there?

The dots start bouncing.

Joaquin: Yeah, she spent the night. Do I even want to know?

Nick: I fucked up, and I need to make it right.

I throw my phone in my cup holder and pull out of the parking lot, speeding across town to get to Sierra. When I finally reach Joaquin's I pull into his driveway, parking right next to her car.

As soon as I reach the front door it swings open, and Joaquin is standing there giving me a disapproving look. "Don't start. Just tell me where she is."

"What the hell did you do, Nick? She's in the bathroom getting sick."

I push past him, heading down the hall to the bathroom, and I hear the sound of her retching. I stop in the doorway, feeling helpless while watching Mona rub her back. Sierra looks up at me right before she leans over the toilet and pukes again.

Her sister stands. "We'll give you guys some privacy." She shuts the door behind her, leaving Sierra and I alone.

Sierra flushes the toilet and stands, waving me

away when I try to help her. "I'm fine. Please stay back." She rinses her mouth and then splashes cold water on her face. "What are you doing here?"

"I went by your apartment, and you weren't there. I texted Joaquin, and he said you were here." I pull her to me, but she tries to pull away. My hand slides down her stomach until I reach the spot where our baby rests. "I'm an asshole."

"I won't argue with that." Sierra crosses her arms, bringing my attention to her tits.

My thumb absently rubs back and forth over her still flat stomach. "You know I didn't mean it when I said that you lead me around by my dick. I was upset when you said we needed to talk, and I just assumed that you were breaking things off with me again."

She turns in my arms and looks up at me with those big blue eyes of hers. "Are you mad about the baby? I'm prepared to do this alone if this isn't something you want." Sierra lets her arms fall to her sides.

I drop down to my knees in front of her and lift Sierra's shirt and pull her boxer's, or my boxers, down enough to expose her lower stomach—where our baby is nestled. Leaning forward I place my lips against her soft skin and wrap my arms around her waist. "How could I be mad?"

I look up at her and see that her eyes are shining with unshed tears. "I don't know why I'm crying." Sierra pulls away from me and rinses out her mouth in the sink. I stand and watch her splash some more water on her face. She dries herself off and turns around to face me. "How do we do this?"

"What do you mean?"

She flushes the toilet and closes the lid before sitting. "I don't know how this all works. You know, this whole co-parenting thing." Sierra's arms rest on her thighs as she stares up at me. I take her in, in all her tattooed beauty.

Before we met I wasn't all that impressed with tattoos on women, but then I laid eyes on her and her sisters—that was all she wrote. Will I ever get one ... maybe, but I wouldn't bet on it.

My girl has two full sleeves; they look like beautiful floral bouquets that go from her shoulders to her wrists. She's got a tribal elephant head on her upper chest. On each ass cheek she's got red lip prints that made me laugh the first time I saw them. On the side of her left thigh she has an owl sitting on a tree limb. The side of the right thigh is a cross that says Mom and Dad.

Her body is most certainly her canvas, and I can't wait to see how it changes as our baby grows. I focus on her last statement. "Baby, I don't want to co-parent. I think we should get married."

Sierra stares at me for a minute and then throws her head back and laughs. I cross my arms and wait for her to finish. "What's so funny?"

She shakes her head. "We're not getting married. We were just having sex. It was just sex." The minute the words leave her mouth she cringes. Sierra jumps up from the toilet. "God, that sounded bad. It's just that we weren't actually even dating ... right?"

"Then let's start dating. We've got seven or so months before the baby comes, so let's date and see what happens."

"What happens if we realize we don't want to be together?" Sierra places a hand on her stomach.

I doubt that is going to happen, but I know there's always been this wall around her that I haven't figured out how to knock down, but I will. I'll show her what an amazing couple we can be if she'd just give us a chance.

"Baby, I don't think that'll happen. But if it did, you and I would do our best to raise our baby together."

Sierra sucks her lower lip into her mouth. Fuck me, she makes my dick hard—like an abnormal amount, and I'm someone who has always loves sex. She lets it go and reaches up, scratching her nose.

"Can we take it slow? I-I haven't been in a serious relationship since college. It didn't end well."

I place my hands on her shoulders. "We can take it as easy as you need to, baby. I have to head to *Nicholas* soon, but have dinner with me tonight. I want to cook for you." I've always had a love for cooking. My parents traveled a lot, and they always took me and my sister, Nadia, with them.

I ate the finest cuisine and developed a refined palate. When I decided I wanted to become a chef, my father threw a fit. He's the top corporate attorney in Atlanta, and that is what he wanted for me.

He got over it, though, when I opened my first restaurant, and it was a huge success. I don't mean to brag, but I've got the Midas touch, and I now own three of the most successful restaurants in and around Atlanta.

These days I don't cook nearly as often as I'd like, but I love cooking for Sierra. She'll try anything and eat it with a lot of sexy enthusiasm. I wouldn't be surprised if this baby was conceived during one of those times. We'd end up eating our food off of each other, but laughing and kissing while we did it.

She smiles up at me, her eyes sparkling, and again she bites that damn lip. "Chicken Picata?" Sierra asks because that's her favorite.

"Anything my baby mama wants." Sierra reaches up to slap me, but I pull her into my arms. "You and I are going to make the prettiest baby," I say against the top of her head. "Your tits are going to be fucking huge... Ah fuck!"

Sierra pinches my side. "Don't call them tits, and you better start watching that mouth. I don't want our baby's first word to be tits or fuck."

I kiss her softly on the mouth. "Stop by the restaurant, and I'll get you a key for my place. You can head on over when you're done at the studio later."

"Okay, I'll see you tonight."

On the way to my car, I find my best friend standing outside waiting for me. "Joaq, I love you, but I don't want any of your shit."

He holds his hands up. "I'm not out here to give you shit. I just wanted to say congratulations. You're having a kid, man. That's so great." Joaquin comes to me, giving me a backslapping hug. The man surprises me when he doesn't let go. "You're going to make a great Dad."

My throat feels thick, and I swear my heart stutters in my chest. "That's only because I've learned from the best." If I'm half the father my best friend is, I'll take it. Neither of us had Dads who were

31

the best role models. His is a philanderer who is on wife number four, and I'm sure working toward screwing that up. Mine is just a fucking snob with a severe sense of entitlement and a wondering eye. Lucky for Joaquin and I, we had my mother who is a freaking saint for putting up with my dad's bullshit.

I climb in my car and make my way toward my restaurant. When I bought it, it was a bar that had gone bankrupt. Getting it for cheap, I was able to put a lot of money into the remodeling of the space and putting in a state of the art kitchen.

Within six months we had a waitlist every Thursday, Friday, and Saturday night. To keep things fresh at all of my restaurants we change the menu every six months. My team is what helps me stay so successful. They never balk when I want to get my hands dirty and jump in the kitchen.

I let myself in the front door and lock it behind me. My shoes slap on the beautiful flooring as I weave through the tables in the dining room. I push through the double doors and make my way down the hall to my office. After I unlock the door I step inside, moving behind my desk.

I go through the bills and the receipts from the last couple of days. My restaurant manager, Keith, is the one who pays all the bills and makes sure everything is on the up and up. I leave everything in the folder ready for him to take care of.

I check the reservations for all three restaurants and see we're booked for dinner service for the weekend. I head back to the kitchen and find my prep cooks prepping for the day.

They're all in culinary school, and I've hired

quite a few graduates to work at my restaurants. I'd love to tell you I hire them all, but I have very high expectations from my team. You have to earn your spot, and some unfortunately just don't make the grade.

I look over everything and then head out to the bar to grab a bottle of water. As I drink it down, I scan the liquor shelf. I only serve top shelf booze in my restaurants. I could choose cheaper shit and still charge what I do, but only serving the best keeps asses in the seats.

Keith arrives an hour later, and we have a quick little meeting in the office. We go over the new menu that we'll start implementing soon. We always close down for a few days for everyone to learn the menu and to taste all of the dishes.

As stressful as it is, I love it because I actually get to do a lot of cooking. "This menu is going to be excellent, Nick."

I'm getting ready to meet with my executive chef when I spot Sierra walking through the front door. Fuck me, she's the most beautiful fucking woman I've ever met. I'm not sure if it's fully hit me yet that my baby is growing inside of her or why it's not scaring me, but it's definitely making me feel something.

I step out from behind the bar and pull her into my arms when she reaches me. "Hey, babe. Are you heading to the studio now?"

"Hey. Yeah, I've got three clients, and the first one is in an hour. I'll be done around nine." I hand her the spare key to my place that I keep in my desk in the office.

"I may or may not be home yet, but just let yourself in and get comfy, and we'll have a late dinner."

I kiss her quickly on the forehead before she leaves.

"Was that your girlfriend?" Keith asks from behind me.

I shrug. "Yes and no. We're working on figuring that out."

"Don't take this the wrong way, but she's not really the kind of woman I picture you…"

"I'm going to stop you right there before you say something that pisses me off." I walk past him into the back, ready to get this day over with.

STENCIL: SUGAR AND SPICE, INK BOOK TWO

SIERRA

I spray and then wipe off the tattoo I just finished. This is the second session we've had. The design is different colored butterflies, and I'm so proud of how it turned out. They look like they're ready to take flight right off her back. She wanted to cover the name of her ex-husband, so we needed a design that would hide it.

Helping her stand, I hand her the handheld mirror, and lead her to the full-length one so she can see it. "Oh my god, Sierra, this is just what I wanted. Thank you." It never gets old seeing the look of pure joy on someone's face when they see their fresh ink.

"I enjoyed working on it. Let's get it covered, and I'll go over your instructions with you." We use a sticky clear sheet instead of plastic wrap. I tell her about leaving it on for twenty-four hours and then take it off and to apply the second plastic sheet after she showers and to leave it for several days.

Mona heard about the stuff, and most of our clients love it. She used it on me when she touched up a tattoo on my foot. I was able to wear shoes and not worry about slathering my tattoo in ointment several times a day.

"If you don't have anyone to apply the new sheet, just call us. You can bring it in, and someone will do it for you."

After I take a quick picture she pays and hugs me one more time before leaving. Lainey cleans my station for me, and I head into the office and grab some crackers. I wash them down with some ginger ale.

"Hey, sis."

I turn to find my baby sister standing in the doorway. "Hey, Heidi Ho."

She rolls her eyes at me. "You know I hate that."

"Why do you think I say it?" I wink at her before grabbing the laptop to upload the pictures of the tattoo I just finished to Instagram. "I have news," I tell her as I set it down. "I'm pregnant. I've known for about a week, but I had it officially confirmed yesterday."

Heidi smiles and runs toward me, wrapping me in her arms. "A baby! That's so great." She kisses my cheek. "I'm assuming it's with that hot hunk of man that you've been boinking on the reg."

"Ugh, you sound like Nick. Don't call it boinking. Yes, it's Nick's baby."

I tell her about him assuming I was going to break things off and then coming to see me at Mona and Joaquin's and then about our plan to "date".

"You know he's in love with you, right?"

37

I shake my head. "What he feels is pure lust, plain and simple."

"Sure, if you say so. He only looks at you like Dad looks at Mom, Joaquin looks at Mona, and the way Colton used to look … well you get the picture." Her eyes turn sad, but she blinks it away.

Before I can say anything to her, she's gone. A twinge of sadness hits me—she and Colton dated from eighth grade through their senior year. They were so cute together, and we all thought they were going to get married and start having babies right after graduation. That didn't happen, and no one really knows what went down, but one day he was just gone, taking my sister's heart with him.

I grab my purse and head out to the front. Heidi gives me a small smile as I pass by as she leads a client to her station. I mime to her to call me tomorrow, and she nods before mouthing congratulations.

Greta's on the computer at the front counter. "Hey, girlie, will you walk me out? I've got to talk to you." I loop my arm through hers as we make our way outside. We stop next to my car. "I just wanted to tell you that I'm pregnant. Nick and I are having a baby." She hugs me, "Don't say anything to Miles because I want to tell him myself."

"Of course. This is so exciting." I kiss her cheek before she heads back inside.

I climb into my car and head toward Midtown where Nick's condo is. His place is gorgeous, and I don't even want to know how much it costs. It's even fancier than Joaquin and Mona's place, and that house is swanky with a capital S. I pull into one of his guest spots and don't see his car, but it could be in his three-car garage.

Inside I greet Alan, the concierge, as I walk toward the hall where the elevators are located. I pull out his key once I reach his floor and let myself inside. I'm always in awe of Nick's home every time I visit. Yes, it's obvious this place costs a lot of money. It's got a state of the art kitchen that I love to watch Nick cook in. The bathrooms are all gorgeous with the basins that sit on top of the vanity and beautiful tiled floors that I swear are heated, but he says they're not. Most of the rooms are wall to wall windows with a view that is picturesque. His bedroom is larger than my apartment with a kick ass king-sized bed. As swanky as it is, it's more comfortable than I expected. I'm not afraid to touch anything, and I would feel comfortable letting my niece and nephew run around and play.

I head into Nick's room and kick off my shoes and grab my phone out of my purse before heading out to the lanai. It's chilly, so I grab one of the cashmere blankets out of the little cubby. There's a perfect view of Ansley Park and the High Museum. I lay on the lounger, and in no time I feel my eyes get heavy.

"Sierra. Sierra, baby, wake up."

I open my eyes to find Nick sitting next to my stomach and his hand caressing my cheek. It's such a tender gesture, and it surprises and warms me at the same time. "Sorry I fell asleep." I slowly sit up, knowing that if I do it too fast it will make my stomach turn. "Did you just get here?"

"Yeah. Come inside and sit in front of the

fireplace. I'll get changed, and then you can keep me company while I cook." He leads me inside, and I curl up in the corner of his sofa facing the fireplace that runs almost the whole length of the room. Nick hands me the remote, and I turn it on.

I rest my head on the cushion as I watch the flames flicker, and once the warmth hits me I feel my eyes getting heavy … again.

Sunlight shines in my face when I blink my eyes open. I feel a big warm body behind me and take a second to just snuggle into him. My belly dips and makes me feel all squishy when I realize his hand is spread wide over my lower belly.

I feel bad because I must've fallen asleep on him again last night. Last thing I remember was curling up on his sofa while he changed his clothes. Nick shifts behind me, and I feel his hard dick digging into my back.

Rolling over slowly and carefully until I'm facing him, I reach out and softly touch his cheek. He's such a beautiful man and looks like he should be in movies. His dark blond hair is swept to the side and still looks styled like it did yesterday. Nick's got a little bit of dark stubble on his face that makes a slight scraping sound as my fingers rub against it.

My skin in comparison to his naturally tanned skin is even paler than it usually is, but that's because I avoid the sun or always cover myself in sunscreen. My tattoos are too colorful to let the sun fade them out. I close my eyes because my stomach starts to turn. I take some deep, cleansing breaths until the feeling passes.

I have to pee, so I slowly slide out of his bed and head into the master bath. It's only then I realize that I'm just in my bra and panties. I shake my head, because I must've been really out to sleep through him undressing me.

After emptying my bladder, I wash my hands. I grab the spare toothbrush I use when I'm here and brush my teeth. Back in the bedroom I slide into bed, lying on my side.

Nick wraps his arm around my waist and pulls me toward him until my back connects with his front. I close my eyes when I feel his lips touch the back of my head.

I open my eyes and squint again because the sun is shining directly into his room. Reaching behind me, I find Nick's side of the bed empty and cold—I must've fallen asleep again. I sit up slowly, breathing in through my nose and out through my mouth as I try to prevent myself from getting sick. I slip out of bed and grab a t-shirt out of Nick's closet—he's the only guy I know who hangs up his t-shirts. Of course some of his t-shirts cost more than my monthly car payment.

Throwing on one of his Atlanta Fire t-shirts, I head down the hall to find him and find him I do. He's at the stove in a pair of basketball shorts that sit low on his narrow hips. Nick turns when he hears me come into the room. "You spoiled my surprise. I wanted to make you breakfast in bed."

He holds out his hand to me, and I take it, letting him pull me toward him. Nick wraps his arms around me. "I looked up online what was safe for you to eat for your morning sickness. I'm making French toast with a strawberry coulis."

"Coulis, huh. It's so sexy when you speak chef to me." I smile up at him.

"Go sit, and I'll bring you a plate."

We sit side-by-side at the counter while we dig into our breakfast. I can't believe he looked online to find out what I could eat. Why does that make me want to swoon and maybe run like hell?

Nick grabs his phone. "When is your next OB appointment?"

"April 20th. Why?"

"I'd like to come with you and meet your doctor." I watch as he adds it to his calendar.

"Why are you being so supportive and not freaking out?" I blurt out, but I need to know. Mona warned me that he was a man hoe, and according to Joaquin he never dated. Before, I found that to be perfect because I didn't want anything more either—the sex was off the charts, and I really liked being around him.

I jerked him around before, I know it, and I honestly can't believe he's being so great right now.

"Why wouldn't I be supportive? You're pregnant with my baby."

"I don't know," I say with shrug. "This is all a lot to take in. My sisters all know. I just need to tell Miles and my parents. Have you told anyone yet?"

Nick picks his coffee up and takes a drink. I'm staring at it lovingly and longingly, and one cup wouldn't hurt me, but I don't think I could stop after one. It's better if I just abstain.

"No, I wasn't sure if I was supposed to wait or not. I mean, I just found out yesterday, but I'll tell my parents and my sister soon."

In the seven months we've been sleeping together, I've never met his sister or his parents. He knows my sisters and brother—at Christmas he met my parents via webcam. Is he embarrassed of me? Where is this insecurity coming from?

My French toast starts to turn in my stomach, and I jump up, running into the bathroom as it comes back up. I get sick over and over until it's just dry heaves, but Nick is there, holding my hair back from my face and rubbing small, comforting circles on my back. "I'm sorry," I say. "I just wasted that delicious breakfast."

"Don't be sorry, baby."

He moves away from me, and then I feel a cold washcloth being placed on my neck. I sigh in relief as I flush the toilet. Resting my cheek on the seat, I close my eyes. "I know this will pass, but not soon enough."

"This morning I was looking online and saw that keeping crackers by your bedside and munching on them before getting out of bed can help ease your stomach. Maybe I should've passed on the French toast."

"No, it was so sweet." I take a deep breath and then slowly stand. I rinse my mouth out and then let him pull me into a hug. "Come take a shower with me?"

Nick smiles, that panty-melting smile of his. "Go get it ready, and I'll be right there." He kisses my forehead and lets me go.

43

In his master bath I brush out my hair and pull it up in a knot. I brush my teeth again and then strip out of my clothes. I love Nick's shower; it's mostly glass with beautiful tile on the one wall with stone flooring. It's got multiple shower nozzles and one in the ceiling that does the whole rain effect.

The warm water feels heavenly as it sluices down my body. I hear the glass door open and feel Nick's large frame press against my back, and his arms wrap around me. "There is nothing I love better than seeing you naked and wet in my shower."

He surprises me by grabbing the soap and begins to slowly wash my body. It's so intimate, and he spends a little extra time soaping up my stomach. His cock is growing hard, but he makes no move to touch me in any sexual way.

Nick squats down as he washes the lower half of my body. He stands back up, and I reach out, wrapping my hand around his dick. I expect him to kiss me or touch me, but instead he grabs my hand and pulls it off of him. Nick kisses the back of it before putting me under the water to rinse me off.

He leads me out of the shower after he shuts the water off. "Aren't you going to wash up?" I ask as he wraps a towel around me.

"I'm going to go workout before I head out to meet Gordo. The Fire's season starts next month, and we're meeting with the coach and his staff today."

Toward the end of last year he was approached to become a co-owner of the Atlanta Fire, our arena football team.

"Okay, I've got to head home and get changed and then run some errands." In his bedroom I throw on my clothes from the day before while I watch Nick out of the corner of my eye as he dresses in black basketball shorts and a sleeveless t-shirt. Fuck, he's sexy. I place my hand on my stomach. If this baby is a boy then I'm going to be in trouble.

Once I'm ready, Nick leads me out, and we ride down the elevator together. He's getting off on the second floor where the fitness room is located, but before he does he gives me a soul searing kiss that makes my toes curl. "Fuck, you're sexy," Nick whispers before he pulls away.

I laugh and swat at him as the doors open. He steps off, and I give him a wave.

A busty blonde approaches Nick with a seductive smile. "Hey, stranger, it's been a long time." But the doors shut before I'm able to see his reaction.

I lean against the back wall as my stomach rolls. I'm not a jealous person, but I'm also not very trusting—especially when it comes to the opposite sex.

It's not lost on me that Nick is hot, and women flock to him. He's never given me a reason not to trust him. That doesn't stop me, however, from wondering if enough temptation is thrown in his face if he'd be rethinking this whole thing and begin dipping into other pools of women.

SIERRA

"Another grandbaby!" my mom squeals through the line—loud enough that I have to pull it away from my ear. "Oh, honey, that's wonderful news. I'm so excited to have another grandbaby to spoil. Do Iris and Max know they have a baby cousin coming?"

I love that my mom and dad already consider Max their grandson, even though they haven't officially met yet.

"No, I mean, maybe Mona and Joaquin told them. I know that I'm not married and this baby wasn't planned, but I'm happy."

"Oh, honey, babies are blessings no matter how they come. What does Nick think, or are we going to have another Sam on our hands?" Even though they've only met through my webcam, I thought they really liked Nick. Before I can defend him, my mom corrects herself. "I'm sorry; that's not fair to Nick. Does he know?"

"Yeah, Mom. He knows. He's happy." I leave out the fact that he thought I was pulling, well, a me. She tells me about their plans to come visit this summer so they can get to know Joaquin and Max better.

When we hang up, I feel better. They have always been supportive of us kids no matter what path we took in our lives. When Mona got pregnant and Sam dumped her, my parents immediately stepped in to help. There was no judgment, only love and support.

Are we like the Brady Bunch, hell no—our parents have always been encouraging no matter what choices we've made.

I grab a can of ginger ale out of my refrigerator and carry it into my bedroom. I'm closing the shop tonight, which means I don't have to be there until four. I'll run my errands before that. The moment I lay down and snuggle in I pass out.

After a three hour nap, I stand in front of my bathroom mirror in a black bra and undies and wash my face, then I do my makeup. Greta Van Fleet blares from my Bluetooth speaker. I'm actually feeling really good right now.

I sipped some of my ginger ale before climbing out of bed, and in the kitchen I munched on some saltines. It seemed to help the nausea, but I wasn't going to get too excited. At any moment it could come back up.

I lean forward as I line my eyes, softly singing *Black Smoke Rising*. I put the lid on the liner tube and grab some powder that gives my cheeks a slight pinkish, dewy glow.

47

I twist up my hair into a bun and then shove bobby pins into it to keep it in place. Giving it a quick spray, I head back into my room and throw on some black leggings, a silver Sugar and Spice, Ink tee, and a hot pink slouchy cardigan. I pull black high-heeled booties out of my closet.

After I slip them on, I stand in front of my full-length mirror. I turn every which way and can admit that I look hot. My curves are subtle, for now, but what will they be like in a few months when I start to show?

When Mona was pregnant with Iris, she stayed pretty tiny and was all belly. Will I be the same, or will I be as big as a house? I don't really exercise— sometimes I'll do yoga with my sister. I hate it, and I whine the whole time.

In the kitchen I pack some snacks and more ginger ale to take with me to the studio. I turn on the nightlight in the hall so when I get home tonight I won't be walking into a dark apartment.

A short while later, I pull into the parking lot of the studio. I grab my lunch bag and purse and head inside. Imagine Dragons is playing through the speakers. Greta is behind the counter, so I'm not surprised she's listening to them; they're her favorite.

She smiles when she looks up and sees me. "You look hot. What's the occasion?"

"I didn't throw up after my nap."

Greta laughs. "Well, okay then. Your five o'clock called a few minutes ago, and he might be late. He has a meeting that may run a bit over."

"Okay, thanks."

In the office I find Iris and Max on the love seat,

watching something on an iPad. "Hey, guys."

"Auntie Sierra!" Iris hops up and runs into my arms. I hug her tight. "Mom says you and Uncle Nick are having a baby."

"Sorry they heard me talking about it," Mona says as she steps into the office.

"That's okay." I look down at my sister's mini me. "Yep, you're going to have a new baby cousin to play with." I kiss the top of her head and then plop down next to Max, wrapping my arm around his shoulders and hugging him to my side. "How was school today, Maximum?"

He smiles up at me. "It was good. They moved Iris to the other side of the classroom. They said we talk too much."

"Well at least you get to stay in the same class." A few minutes later, Joaquin enters the room and goes to my sister, pulling her into his arms. They share a kiss that makes me smile. Iris jumps up and runs right to her Joaq, who has been more of a father to her then that idiot, Sam.

I love that he picks Iris up and hugs her tightly. When he sets her down, Max gives his dad a hug. I step out of the office and let them have some privacy.

They all leave while I'm setting up my station for my appointment. I print out the picture of the tattoo my client wants and the colors he decided on. Normally if someone brings in a design they pulled off the Internet, I add my touches to it to make it unique.

Heidi is at her station working on a foot tattoo. She's in her zone, and she pretty much blocks everyone out. Out of all of us she is the one who doesn't really talk while she works, but most of her clients know how she works, and they bring earbuds—listening to music, watching movies, or listening to audiobooks.

I hear the bell from above the door and turn to find my appointment walking in. "Hey, Nate." I hold out my hand to him, and he gives it a quick shake.

"Sorry I was late."

"No problem at all. I've got everything ready to go. Have a seat, and can I get you a soda or bottle of water?" I ask as we head toward my station.

He shakes his head. "No, thanks; I'm good."

We get started, and it takes me three hours before we're done with the outline. He'll come back in three weeks, and I'll work on colors and shading. I check my phone and see a text from Nick.

Nick: Hey, babe, how are you feeling? I know you're working, but can I bring you dinner?

That warm feeling in my chest comes back. I quickly type a response.

Sierra: I brought my dinner, but if you wanted to come hang out with me I wouldn't say no.

The black dots start bouncing again.

Nick: I'll see you in about an hour.

My next appointment shows up early, and it's a quick one, just a song title on her forearm. It's Pink Floyd's *Shine On You Crazy Diamond* in her favorite aunt's handwriting.

She began to cry while I did it, and she told me that her aunt had passed away a month earlier after a long battle with breast cancer.

As I wipe it off and go over aftercare

instructions with her, I blink back the tears that threaten to spill because apparently pregnancy turns me into a big cry baby. She pays and gives me a nice tip and a big hug before she leaves.

I've got about ten or fifteen minutes before Nick gets here, so I head into the office and sit on the love seat, taking a drink of my ginger ale.

My stomach gets queasy, and I close my eyes and begin to breathe deep and slow. With a hand resting on my lower abdomen, I whisper, "Baby, this nausea has got to stop. Your mommy is tired of living off saltines and ginger ale."

The feeling eventually passes, and I open my eyes to find Nick standing in the doorway watching me with a soft smile on his beautiful face. "You okay?"

"Yeah, just nauseated."

Nick joins me on the love seat. "I feel bad. I'm the reason you feel sick, but it'll be worth it in the end, right?" He places his hand on my lower stomach and leans forward. "Hey, baby boy, this is your dad. Could you take it easy on your momma?"

I smile because he thinks this baby's a boy. I'm willing to bet that it's a girl. Before I can stop myself my fingers sift through Nick's hair, my nails scratching against his scalp. My nipples tingle when he does this throaty growl, and I can feel it all the way down to my nether regions.

He looks up at me and leans in until his lips chastely touch mine. Before I can even kiss him, he's pulling away. Now I want to growl because I want more.

I stand to grab my lunch bag and bring it back to

the love seat. Nick pulls out a box from his paper bag, and I groan because it's a mixture of sushi from my favorite sushi place, Eight Sushi.

"That's really mean. I can't eat sushi right now."

He holds my gaze as he shoves a piece into his mouth. I do the same as I shove a stupid cracker into mine, and then I moan around it, spitting cracker crumbs everywhere. Nick laughs and wraps his arm around my shoulder, pulling me into his side.

While we eat, Heidi comes sauntering in. "Well hey, baby daddy. Congratulations."

Nick stands and hugs my sister. "Thanks, sweetheart."

She turns to me. "Your last appointment cancelled, and the dick tried to ask for his deposit back. I reminded him that all deposits are non-refundable. He hung up on me."

We require a $100 deposit because if they don't show up for their appointments that's money we lose. Nine times out of a ten we won't get a walk-in to take that spot.

Normally people don't squawk at the deposit, but every now and then one asshole does. "Add him to the do-not reschedule book." We started keeping track of people who are rude, nasty, and don't comply by our terms and conditions. This is our business, our livelihood, and we're not taking shit from anyone.

"It'll be my extreme pleasure to add him," Heidi says before flouncing out of the office.

"No one has ever gotten violent with you guys, have they?" Nick asks while looking at me closely.

I shake my head. "Not ever. People complain about the deposit, but that's it."

Luckily he drops it, and we finish our dinner. I stand once I'm finished and grab a peppermint out of my purse. Nick comes up behind me and wraps his arms around me. "What time are you done here?"

"Ten. Why?"

He moves my hair to one side and kisses my neck. "I'll be back to get you. I want you to pack a bag and stay at my place. We'll have lunch on Sunday with my mom and sister, and we can tell them about the baby."

Wow, okay … that's kind of a big deal. I've never met his parents or sister before. Of course, the couple of times he's tried to get me to meet them I've come up with excuses not to.

Now, things are different—hell, they were different before, and I just chose to ignore that fact. Regardless of what happens we'll still be raising this baby together. "Okay, that sounds nice."

Nick turns me in his arms and leans down, kissing me. I really wish he'd kiss me like he used to and yes, a lot of times it would lead to sex, but dammit I miss those deep, passionate kisses. "I'll see you in a couple of hours."

Just like that he's gone.

NICK

After leaving Sierra I head back to my place to get changed and do a little work before I meet her back at the studio. Gordo was going to be sending me an email with the information on the new quarterback for the team.

I head into my bedroom and change into a pair of jeans and a blue thermal long sleeved shirt. After I throw my shoes on, I head into my office and boot up my laptop.

Colton Winters is the QB for NY. It's risky to consider bringing a new QB into the team right now, but after reading through all of his stats, his record speaks for itself, and we'd be stupid not to sign him. Plus, it looks like he's originally from here and was the star QB for his high school.

The guy had a promising future in football, but then it was like he dropped off the face of the planet.

I send Gordo a quick email telling him he was

smart to snag him now while we have the chance. Hopefully, he'll fit in with his teammates and can prove his worth.

Gordo's online because he responds immediately that he's making the call now and flying him down here to meet with us this week. I'm curious as to why he's leaving a team that he's got an exceptional record with. This could be good marketing as well: Hometown golden boy returns to where it all began.

A few hours later Sierra and I are walking into my place, and she's got her small rolling suitcase. I watch her ass as she walks through the foyer and feel my dick twitch.

This woman has me thinking about sex all of the time, but now knowing that my baby is in her belly I'm scared to touch her. I'm not only talking about my dick, but I'm almost a whole foot taller than her. I could hurt her, or them.

I follow her into my bedroom and take her suitcase from her, sticking it in the closet. Sierra's sitting on the end of my bed when I come out. "Do you want to watch a movie?" I hold my hand out to her.

"Sure." She places her hand in mine. We head into the living room, and I sit down before pulling her down onto my lap. I grab the remote and scan through the movies.

Sierra is the only woman I know who loves horror movies as much as I do. Her favorite is on Netflix, so I turn on The Conjuring. She falls sleep on me almost immediately. I situate us so we're on our sides, and Sierra's back is snug against my front. She fits me so perfectly, like she was made just for me.

When my eyes start to feel heavy, I don't fight it.

I open my eyes and see that it's barely dawn. Sierra is snoring softly in front of me. Carefully, I slide out from behind her and then slowly lift her into my arms.

She doesn't move or stir as I carry her to my room or when I take her leggings off, leaving her in a t-shirt and panties. I strip down to my boxer briefs and climb in next to her, pulling her back into my arms. In no time I fall back asleep.

I brace myself with one hand on the shower wall and wrap the other around my cock. This morning I woke up with Sierra wrapped around me like a spider monkey, and I could feel the heat coming from her pussy.

I wanted nothing more than to pull her panties to the side and sink inside her, but I'm scared to hurt her or our baby. I know it's irrational and probably impossible, but I really want to hear it from the doctors themselves that it's not possible.

Instead of fucking that beautiful creature in my bed, I settle for my own hand, and as I begin to pump my dick my thoughts are all about her. My dick is hard as fuck as I remember the time that I laid her out on my kitchen island, covered her body in whipped cream, and then licked every little bit off.

I groan as that tingling feeling begins to build at the base of my spine, and several other images of us fucking flash through my mind as I pick up speed, jerking my dick faster and faster.

My eyes roll back as my cum shoots out of my dick, splashing all over the tile wall. I quickly rinse off and then step out of the shower. I freeze when I find Sierra standing in the doorway. "Good morning." Shit, how much did she see?

"Morning," she mumbles before turning away and heading into my room.

"Shit," I say quietly.

I quickly shave and then run a little bit of product through my hair. With my towel wrapped around my waist I head into my bedroom and find Sierra in my closet going through her suitcase. She comes out with clothes in her hands and then lays the outfit on my bed.

Sierra walks right by me and goes into the bathroom, shutting the door behind her. "Fuck." She saw me jerking off and is now pissed.

The water turns on, and I go to enter the bathroom, but find the door locked.

She is obviously hurt or pissed. I hear a noise and put my ear to the door—is she crying? That idea is quickly squashed when I hear her moan, and my dick perks up at that beautiful sound.

Like the pervert I am, I stand at the door with my ear against it and listen. It doesn't take long before I hear her cry out. I reach down squeezing my dick, willing it to go down.

I busy myself changing into a pair of black Rag and Bone slim-fit chinos and a gray Tom Ford poplin dress shirt. After I tuck in my shirt, I put on my black leather belt. I slip my feet into a pair of black Bruno

Magli leather loafers.

I head into the kitchen and make a cup of coffee. While that brews, I eat a banana. In the distance I can hear a hair dryer going. Today we're having brunch with my mom and sister. I'm a little nervous because I've never brought a woman home to meet them.

There's never been anyone I've been that serious about. Sierra changed that. Whether she believes it or not, I have thought we had something special since the first time I touched her. Now she's giving me something I never thought I wanted ... a baby, our child.

I open my iPad and pull up the news app and am reading an article when I hear the click clack of heels on the floor. When Sierra steps into the kitchen, I want to swallow my tongue.

Sierra's platinum locks are in a deep side part and in loose curls. Her upper lid is lined in black, and her lashes look long and lush. Her cheeks are a tinted mauve and on her lips are a cotton candy pink color.

She's got diamond studs in her ears and a beautiful silver necklace around her neck. Her black cashmere sweater molds to her gorgeous breasts. She's wearing gray jeggings that are so sexy on her, and the high-heeled black booties make her legs look super long.

Sierra marches right to me, stopping in front of me. "Why won't you fuck me? Does the idea of me pregnant with your baby repulse you?"

I shake my head. "I find you sexier than ever. You make my dick hard whenever I look at you—whenever I think about you."

"Then why haven't you touched me? Sure,

58

you've kissed me, but that's all you've done. You jerked off in the shower rather than touch me." She tries to hide the hurt from me, but I can see it in her eyes.

I grab her hands in mine. "I know this sounds crazy, but I don't want to hurt you or our baby."

Sierra rolls her eyes at me. "You know that's impossible, right? I mean, yeah your dick is big, but the baby is well protected in there. If we're still sleeping together when I'm showing, then I'm sure we'll have to get creative, but I'm pregnant, not injured."

"I'm gonna ignore the "if we're still sleeping together" comment, and you're right." I let go of one of her hands and wrap my hand around the back of her neck. "Tonight I'll cook for you since I didn't the other night because you fell asleep, and we'll have a romantic night."

I lean down and kiss her. "You look so fucking beautiful."

"You're not so bad yourself." Sierra rests her hands on my chest. "I hope your mom and sister like me."

"They'll love you. I'm sure of it." I grab my keys, wallet, phone and then Sierra's hand. She's quiet as we ride the elevator down. When the doors slide open, I lead her out with a hand on the small of her back.

We reach my car, and I open the door for her, and her light floral scent wraps around me when I slide in my seat. We head toward *Bistro Niko*. I'm sure my mother is there already and will give me shit for being "late" which means at least ten minutes early.

Our reservation was made for eleven, but if they don't have our table ready when she gets there, she gets an attitude. Usually I'll slip the host or hostess a tip just as a "I'm sorry my mother is a pain in the ass" gesture.

When I pull into the parking lot, I park and come around helping Sierra out. I wrap my arm around her waist and lead her toward the doors. As soon as we step inside, I scan the dining area and spot my mother and sister at a table by the window.

My sister stands as we approach. She's two years younger than my twenty-nine years. Nadia looks just like me: dark blonde hair, blue eyes, and naturally-tan skin. She's tall for a woman, standing at five-feet-ten inches tall.

Both of us get our height from our dad. Our mom is shorty compared to us.

"Hey, big brother."

I let go of Sierra and wrap my arms around my sister. "Hey, Nadia, you look beautiful as always. I want you to meet my girlfriend, Sierra. Sierra this is my baby sister, Nadia."

"It's a nice to meet you, Nadia." Sierra holds her hand out, and my sister looks at it and then sighs before taking it in hers. I give her a look that I hope conveys that I'm not happy.

I turn Sierra toward my mother. "Baby, this is my mother, Jessica. Mother, this is Sierra."

My mom smiles widely at Sierra. "It's so nice to meet you. Aren't you pretty as a picture?" Have I mentioned that my mom is a true Southern belle, because she totally is? "Nicholas, don't you call me

Mother. That sounds so pretentious."

Mom pulls Sierra into a hug and then kisses both cheeks.

"It's nice to meet you, Mrs. Echols."

I pull out Mom and Sierra's chairs and push them in when they sit. I sit next to Nadia as our waiter brings us waters and my mom orders us a round of mimosas. Opening my mouth, I go to tell my mom that Sierra's pregnant, but the words don't come out.

"Sierra, tell me, what is it that you do?" my mom asks her.

"My sisters and I own a tattoo studio." Sierra grabs her water, taking a sip. "Ahem, I'm a tattoo artist."

I cut in to add, "She does incredible work. Their studio is famous, and they even were asked to do a reality show, but they said no."

"Why would you want to say no to an opportunity like that? It could make you famous." Nadia asks as she flips her hair over her shoulder.

"We don't want to be exploited just because we're women. Plus, they'll want for us to create drama to keep people watching, and that's not the type of image we want to have."

Our waiter brings our drinks, and I casually move Sierra's in between us. She flashes me a small smile.

"Do you have tattoos?" Mom asks her.

Sierra grabs her phone out of her purse and quickly swipes at it. "These are my tattoos." She hands my mom her phone, and I watch my mother for her reaction.

"They're very beautiful, but I don't really

61

understand why someone would want to mark their body forever." Mom hands Sierra's phone to my sister who glances at the screen and then hands it back.

"Yeah, definitely not my thing." Nadia looks at me and shrugs.

SIERRA

Our waiter comes to take our order, and I'm happy to have the brief reprieve from the judgment going on right now. I'm uncomfortable and just want to go home.

I'm used to people reacting to my ink the way Nick's mom and sister both did. I was really expecting or hoping to get along with Nadia, but she's being snooty toward me.

When the waiter asks me for my order, I order the Brioche French Toast and a hot tea.

"You're not drinking?" his mom asks.

I look to Nick because I don't know what to say, and he doesn't open his mouth, so I turn to her. "I have to babysit my niece and nephew later, so I shouldn't really drink."

Jessica nods. "Yes, of course. I hear that your sister is living with Joaquin and Max. How is that going?"

"I think it's going really well. They all seem to be really happy." I smile at her.

"I can't believe you and Joaquin gave up your man ho ways," Nadia says as she looks at her brother.

This bitch, and I'll say it because she's acting like one, is trying to push my buttons. Nick surprises me by standing and grabbing his sister's arm. "Come with me, now."

She stands and reluctantly follows her brother.

"I apologize for my daughter. She's spoiled and also loves her brother very much. Nadia's just a little overprotective."

"No need to apologize," I tell her. She asks to see some more pictures of my ink so I show her, and I also show her pictures of some of the tattoos I've done.

"You do beautiful work. Do you paint or draw on canvas?" She flips through the photos and stops at a picture I took of Iris and Max. "They're so adorable, and he looks so much like his dad."

"He does, and Iris is my sister's mini me too. The kids are so close it'll be neat to watch as they get older."

Nick and Nadia come back and both take a seat just as they bring our food. Jessica ordered something with salmon in it because the smell hits me, and my stomach immediately turns.

I cover my mouth with my napkin and take a slow, deep breath, silently praying that no one at the table notices.

"My goodness, Sierra, are you okay? You look a little green around the gills," his mom asks as she looks at me closely and then looks at Nick. "Ar-are you pregnant?" Jessica whispers it like it's a bad word.

Nick reaches across the table, grabbing my hand. "Yes, Mom. Sierra's having my baby."

Jessica gets very quiet and doesn't look up from her plate. "I-I think I need a minute. If y'all excuse me." She gets up like her ass is on fire and heads toward the restrooms.

Nadia stands. "I'll go check on her." Nick stops his sister. "No, I'll go." I can feel his sister's eyes on me, but I don't dare look at her right now. Of course, without her brother here she jumps on me instantly.

"Well, how'd you do it? Poke holes in the condoms? Tell him you were on birth control? He's slept with half of Atlanta and has managed to not knock anyone up before now." My stomach turns, and my eye begins to twitch, which happens when I'm mad.

I look at her, and she's wearing a nasty smirk on her face. What I want to do is dive over the table and punch Nadia, but instead I grab my phone and order an Uber. I'm not going to stay here and be made to feel bad.

I pull out my wallet and throw a twenty on the table, get up, and walk away. Weaving my way through the restaurant, I feel relief wash over me as I see the doors up ahead.

Once I'm outside, I shake out my hands because my palms are sweating and trembling. My car shows up, and I climb in. I send a quick text to Nick.

Sierra: Sorry I left, but I wasn't going to sit and listen to your sister accuse me of getting pregnant on purpose.

I hold my phone on my lap, and when it chimes, I turn it over and read Nick's text.

Nick: Where are you?

Sierra: I'm heading back to your place.

The dots bounce.

Nick: I'll meet you there. I'm so fucking sorry.

The driver drops me off, and I pull my keys out, heading inside. I'm just grabbing a bottle of water when I hear the front door open. "Sierra," Nick calls out.

"In the kitchen."

As soon as he comes around the corner he comes right to me, pulling me into a big hug. "That was not the way it was supposed to go down."

"Nick, it's not your fault. I'm sorry I left, but I wasn't going to listen to the bullshit she was saying." I shake my head. "I'm so sick and tired of people treating my sisters and me like trash because we're covered in tattoos."

I take a drink of my water. "I'm so tired of it always being the woman's fault when she ends up pregnant. If memory serves it takes both a man and a woman to make a baby."

"Baby, you don't need to say anything. My mom will come around and even if she doesn't, I wouldn't give a fuck. We made a baby, a baby that is going to be beautiful like his or her momma. A baby that is equal parts you and me. We're in this together, and I honestly don't give a shit if people are happy or mad about it because I'm ecstatic."

I grab his face and pull him down until our lips are inches apart. "Thank you for saying that."

Our lips meet in a slow glide, but Nick pulls away, and disappoint fills me. I step back to walk away from him. He stops me, grabs the water bottle out of my hands, and picks me up—my legs hug his hips.

Nick, Mr. Always Talking, doesn't say anything as we move through his home. When my back hits the bed, Nick moves us until my head hits the pillows.

He leans in close. "I don't want you to ever thank me for defending and protecting my woman and my child." Nick kisses me again, and the moment his tongue touches my lips, I immediately open to him.

Our tongues dance as he hovers over me. I know he's being mindful of the baby, but I want—no I need—to feel his weight on me.

I reluctantly stop kissing him. "You're not going to hurt either one of us. Stop being gentle ... please."

Reaching between us, I place my hand on his hard dick. Even through his pants I can feel it jump. That's all I need to do before he lays in between my legs, attacking my mouth with vigor.

He pushes up, but only to pull my sweater off. With quick fingers I unbutton his shirt, and then he shrugs it off, followed by my undershirt. Nick leans down and kisses me slowly before his lips begin to travel down my neck.

I moan as he nips the tender flesh of my neck. He continues to trail his lips down my neck, my throat, and pulls the cups of my bra down, sucking one nipple and then the other into his mouth. They're super sensitive right now, and I can feel each suck all the way down to my pussy.

He lets his free hand slide down my belly and then into panties. Nick groans against my breast and whispers against my skin, "Your cunt is always so wet for me."

"Yes," I moan as I arch my neck. "Finger me please." He does what I want and need. I cry out as first one finger than another enters me. Nick pumps them in and out, rubbing that magical spot inside of me.

He works his way down my body and stops at my stomach as he kisses around my navel. He looks up at me and gives his panty-melting smile. Nick removes his fingers from me and licks them clean, moaning as he does it.

After removing my jeggings and panties, he removes his pants and boxer briefs before he climbs in between my legs. "Lean up, baby," he tells me, and then I feel him unhook my bra, tossing it somewhere on the floor.

Nick does a lazy perusal of my body and runs his hand down from my neck to my stomach and then back up. "You take my breath away."

He kisses me again and immediately I open my mouth to him, and our tongues tangle. Nick reaches down and spreads my legs wider before sinking his cock inside of me.

I moan long and loud as he fills me. I swear he was made for me, and I was made for him. As soon as he's buried balls deep inside me he freezes. "Fuck, you feel so good." I ripple around him as he stares at me with a look on his face that scares me, yet excites me.

"Please move," I beg.

Nick grabs both of my arms and then pins them by my wrists to the bed. Painfully slow he pulls almost all of the way out before he thrusts back inside. He hits my clit with each thrust and then he gets up more on his knees and begins to roll his hips in a way that hits all the good spots inside of me.

He leans down and sucks one nipple into his mouth and then the other, working them both until I ache with the desire to come so bad it hurts. I can't move. I'm at his mercy, but I fucking love it.

He does a little grinding thrust that takes me from zero to sixty in about two seconds. I come so hard my whole body shakes, and he begins to pound into me at a punishing pace.

He groans against my chest as he shudders against me. I feel it as Nick bathes my channel in his cum. When my orgasm starts to lessen in intensity, I'm able to pull my arms out of the shackles of Nick's hands.

I wrap my arms around his head, and I'm sure he can feel my heart racing, but I don't care. His breath hits me in rapid puffs as he pants against my breasts.

I whimper as he pulls his softening cock out of me. "Stay here. I'll be right back." I roll to my side and watch Nick walk naked into his bathroom.

He returns a minute later with a washcloth in his hand. "Let me clean you up, baby." Nick gently wipes between my legs and then tosses the washcloth into the hamper.

He climbs into bed with me and leans over my body and presses his lips to my lower stomach. "Hey, baby, this is your daddy. I love you so much already."

My heart races, and butterflies take flight in my belly. I slide my fingers through his hair until he looks up at me and smiles. My stomach chooses this moment to make it known that I haven't eaten yet.

"Let's get you fed, baby." He grabs me a t-shirt of his and slips it over my head. Nick throws on a pair of basketball shorts. He scoops me up in his arms and carries me out to the kitchen and sets me on a barstool at the island.

He makes me a cup of tea, and I watch as he doctors it up the way I like—with a little bit of milk and honey. Nick sets it down in front of me and makes himself a cup of coffee. I ask him something that I'm afraid of the answer. "How was your mom?" I take a sip of my tea and look up at him.

"She's not happy. Nothing like a mom lecturing her almost thirty-year-old about safe sex." He leans against the granite island top. "She wants us to consider getting married before you start to show. When we got back to the table, I got your text about Nadia. I told her I was too fucking pissed to talk, but she and I would have words later."

I reach across the counter and grab his hand. "I'm sorry."

Nick shakes his head. "No, you have nothing to be sorry for. I got you pregnant, and I'm fucking thrilled. Is it the best timing? No, it's not, but I will never regret this."

I begin to cry, and I want to blame it on hormones, but instead I cry because I'm lucky to have a father for my baby who wants to be involved. Who I know will no doubt love our baby with all he's got.

Nick comes around and wraps his arms around

me. His bare chest is hard, smooth, and the perfect place to rest my cheek. While I cry, he rubs my back slowly, up and down until the tears begin to slow and then eventually stop.

I look up into his handsome face. "I'm sor—"

He puts a hand over my mouth. "Stop apologizing."

My stomach starts to turn a little bit. I take a slow breath and will the nausea to stop.

"Can I do anything?" he asks. Fuck, if I'm not careful I'm going to totally fall in love with him, and for me that leads to heartache—no thank you.

"No, I'm good. It'll pass in a minute. What's on the agenda today for you?" I ask.

"I just need to stop by the restaurants and meet with the managers to set up our next meeting. What about you?" He reaches out and brushes a platinum curl out of my face.

"I should call Miles before one of my sisters accidentally tells him I'm pregnant before I get the chance to do it. I think that's it." I cover my mouth as I yawn widely and loudly. "Maybe I'll take a nap first. Do you mind?" Napping is now a priority above eating.

Nick shakes his head. He scoops me up in his big, strong arms and carries me into his bedroom and lays me down. I burrow under the covers, and it doesn't take long before I'm asleep.

EVAN GRACE

NICK

It's been two weeks since I found out that Sierra is carrying my baby. We've managed to stave off the morning sickness, but she's still nauseated a lot. Especially if she smells something bad, which means I use a bathroom far away from her when I have to … well, you know.

Today Gordo and I are meeting with Stan, the coach of the Fire and Colton our new QB. From the reports that Stan has sent us, Colton is fitting in with the team, and they seem to be working together well.

The real test will be when the season starts. I pull into the parking lot of Verizon Stadium. I use my badge to get me in the side door that the athletes and staff use. Down the hall I find Gordo on his phone.

I clap him on the shoulder before stepping into the office and find Coach sitting in a chair next to a man with light brown hair.

They see me and both stand. "Hey, Stan, good to

see you again." We share a half-handshake, half-backslapping hug. I step back and turn to the large man next to him.

He's got to be at least six-feet-four or five. He's built like Tom Brady, lean and strong looking. "Colton, it's good to finally meet you. I'm Nick Echols."

"It's good to meet you." His grip is strong, confident—I like that.

Once Gordo joins us, we start talking about Colton's future with us. We watch some of his game footage, and honestly if an NFL team doesn't come knocking on his door soon I'll be surprised. This guy is absolutely amazing and has got a natural gift.

Before we all take our leave, I tell them that our plan is to have a team party at one of my restaurants before the season starts. It'll be for players, coaching staff, trainers and family. We'll serve hors d'oeuvres and cocktails.

"I'll send out formal invites later this week. I have a couple of friends with the local media outlets, and I'll invite them to come as well."

Stan and Colton leave first, leaving Gordo and I alone. "Fuck, man, he's fucking talented," I tell him.

"I told you. I can guarantee that if he plays as well as he did last year, the NFL teams will come beating down his door."

We decide to take a look around and make sure our advertisers' signage is clearly visible while the dance team is on the field practicing. They're beautiful women, I won't lie, but they don't hold a candle to the platinum blonde who stole my fucking heart.

"Hi, Nick," Staci, the lead dancer/cheerleader, coos. I know she's got a thing for me, but I won't go there—no matter how hard she flirts. She twirls an auburn curl around her finger as she comes walking over. "You're looking good."

"Thanks, Stace. How are the routines coming along?" She is an amazing dancer. That's why she's the head cheerleader.

"They're coming right along. We've got an amazing group of girls." Staci bites her lower lip and smiles at me. "Have a drink with me tonight."

The old me would jump all over that, spending days between her thighs, but why would I want hamburger when I've got beef tenderloin at home? I shake my head. "I appreciate the offer, but I'll have to pass." I smile and walk over to Gordo who is waiting by the doors.

"You're not going to hit that?"

I haven't told him how serious I am about Sierra, not that I'm ashamed or anything, but I want to keep things private. I give him a pointed look.

"I forgot. Are you still seeing that tattooed girl?"

"Her name is Sierra, and yes, we're still together." I look at him as we walk through the door. "If I have it my way we're going to be serious, really fucking serious."

He wears a shocked look on his face. I can understand why—my reputation is definitely that of a ladies man, player, or womanizer. The last one I don't like because I've never led someone on. I was always up front about the fact that I didn't do serious.

"Wow. Well no wonder you said no to Staci."

I shake my head. "Don't stick your dick in any

of that. You fuck the wrong girl, and she could fuck up your career. Monogamy isn't a bad thing."

As he walks me out, we discuss the party and our party budget. I tell him we should have the party at my steakhouse, *Blaze*, because I have a whole second level that's for parties. It even has its own entrance.

"I'll have my assistant email you a mockup of the invites and then we'll get those in the mail," I tell him.

"Great, let's talk this week about the food, and I'll send you my contribution." It won't be much because I know Gordo's hurting financially; that's why he brought me in.

We exchange a backslapping hug, and I leave. I decide to stop by Sierra's studio and find the parking lot full. I'm not surprised, though, because everyone wants their ink done by one of the Collins sisters.

Two girls are sitting on the chaise lounge in the waiting area looking at an iPad. Lainey is sitting behind the front desk. She smiles when I step up to the counter. "Hey, Lainey. How are you doing, doll?"

"Hi, Nick. As you can see Sierra's busy, but Miles is in the office waiting for Heidi if you want to hang out with him. I'll send Sierra back when she's done."

I give a knock on the desk and give Mona a chin lift as she waves at me. In their office I find the only male Collins sibling typing away on his laptop. The artistic gene definitely touched all of them in one way or another.

"What's up, Miles?"

He looks up when I sit across from him. "Hey,

man. Shit's good. How about yourself?" I reach across, shaking his hand.

I tell him about the party and that he's invited. "Bring Victoria with you." I'm not sure what's going with him and Joaquin's cousin, who is like a sister to me, but they've been spending a lot of time together.

"Yeah, I might do that. My sister told me about the baby and that you guys are dating."

We've always gotten along, and I hope that carries over to now. I nod. "Doing things a little backward, but I've always had a tendency to do things the way I want."

Miles smiles at me. "It'll be good for Sierra—keep her on her toes." He shuts his laptop, shoving it into a bag. Looking up at me, his face is serious … hard. "If you hurt my sister, I will kill you. I'm a writer who has done a lot of research on disposing of bodies." Miles stands and comes around, clapping me on the shoulder. "See you later."

I can only shake my head. "See ya." I wave at Heidi who meets her brother in the mouth of the hall.

While I wait for Sierra I send Geoff, my assistant, my ideas for the invitations. He's a graphic design whiz and tells me he'll get right on it. I wouldn't be surprised if the mockup lands in my email tonight.

"Hey." I look up and find Sierra standing in the doorway, looking so fucking gorgeous. She's wearing a ruby red Sugar and Spice, Ink slouchy t-shirt that hangs off of one shoulder. Sierra's wearing black jeggings with rips up and down her legs, and on her feet a short pair of black motorcycle boots.

I signal with a wiggle of my finger to come to

me, and she does. I grab her hand and have her straddle my lap. Holding her by her hips, I smile up at her beautiful face.

"Hey yourself. How are you feeling?" I pull her face down, kissing her softly.

"Good, just tired. I have one more appointment, and then I can leave. Mona swears in another month and a half or so I'll feel like a million bucks. I can't wait for that." She covers her mouth as she yawns.

"Can't you cancel your last appointment?"

She shakes her head. "I'm okay. It's only going to be like an hour or so. I do need to sleep at my place tonight. I've hardly been there, and I am sure I need to clean it."

"Fine, I'll head home and pack a bag. I can either meet you there or meet you here."

"You don't have to stay at my place. My bed is a lot smaller than yours," Sierra says and then moves to stand, but I stop her. "What?"

I reach up, cupping her cheek. "I'm staying with you. I like waking up with you all snuggled up against me in the morning, and I like feeling your ass against my cock. I like starting my morning listening to the little moans you make while I pluck your nipples and finger your pussy."

Sierra's cheeks look flushed, and her pupils dilate. She smacks my chest and laughs. "You're such a pig." She sighs. "Fine, I'll give you my spare keys, and I'll meet you there. When I'm done, do you want me to grab dinner?"

"No, I'll cook for you."

"But you always cook for me."

I shrug. "Baby, I'm a chef above all else. I love

78

cooking, and I love cooking for you even more."

"Stop being so sweet." She strokes my lip with her thumb. "I thought we were just dating? We seem to be moving at Mach five."

"There are no set rules, baby. All I know is that what I want to build with you is…"

"Oh shit, I'm sorry." Lainey stands in the doorway. "Your next appointment is here. I got her a bottle of water, and she's sitting at your station." She disappears as quickly as she appeared.

I let Sierra go, and she grabs the spare keys from the desk and comes back to me. "What are you making me for dinner?"

I stand and stick her keys in my pocket. "It's a surprise, but you know it'll be delicious." I kiss her on the lips quickly before heading out.

EVAN GRACE

SIERRA

I slip on the black midi dress that hits right at my knees. It skims over my curves and shows off my breasts, that are starting to look bigger, and the very tiny baby bump that I have. The long sleeves cover most of my tattoo sleeves, but they do peek out from under them.

Tonight is the party for The Atlanta Fire, their coaching staff, and the rest of the people involved. Nick left earlier to make sure everything was ready. He was lucky I was in the shower when I left or I might've jumped him.

Nick was wearing dark gray slacks that showed off his muscular thighs and tight ass. His black dress shirt was opened at the collar. His suit jacket fit him like a glove.

He opened the shower door, and I met him at the opening for a goodbye kiss.

Now I smooth down my dress. I slip on a couple

of necklaces, bracelets, and diamond earrings. My platinum hair is in curls that give me a modern Marilyn Monroe look. I spray my hair one more time before slipping on a pair of red spiked heel booties.

My phone rings, and I see that it's Mona. I'm catching a ride with her and Joaquin.

"Hey, sissy," I answer.

"Hey, Momma, we're here. Do you want me to send Joaquin up?"

I hold my cell phone by my shoulder while I shove my powder and lipstick in my red candy skull clutch. "No, that's okay. I'm ready, and I'll be right down." I hang up and stick my phone in my bag.

After locking up, I take the elevator down and head out the doors toward Joaquin's Range Rover. He hops out, looking handsome in a fitted black suit and blue dress shirt.

Always the gentleman, he opens the back door for me and helps me inside. We reach *Blaze*, and Joaquin pulls up at the valet. I climb out and stand on the sidewalk while my sister climbs out.

She looks so pretty with her gray/purple hair in a chignon. Her dress is like mine but gray. Mona's wearing the pink diamond studs that Joaquin bought her for Christmas.

When Joaquin wraps his arm around Mona's waist, she smiles up at him, and my eyes burn. I'm so fucking happy for her, and after what Sam put her through I'm glad she's got a man who loves her as fiercely as Joaquin does.

Joaquin opens the door for us, and we head up a beautifully polished wood staircase. We reach the top, and I'm in awe. The space is all soft lighting, dark wood, and music.

Woman and Men in black pants and white shirts walk around with little silver trays. We step inside the room, and there are quite a few people. I scan the room looking for Nick.

In the corner I find him and the other owner with women in very tiny dresses standing around them. Nick throws his head back, laughing loudly at something a redhead says to him.

He spots me, and his face splits into a wide grin. Nick comes toward us and pulls me into his arms and kisses me deeply. He pulls back enough to look me over. "Damn, you're the sexiest woman I've ever seen."

I hear the redhead who was talking to him a minute ago mutter a, "Yeah, right."

"Thank you," I tell him quietly.

He wraps his arm around my waist as he greets my sister and Joaquin. He turns back to me. "Where is everyone else?"

"They should be here anytime. Are your parents coming?" We haven't talked about his family since the morning we had brunch. I know he's spoken to them, but there have been no arrangements to meet his dad at this point, so I don't know what's going to happen there.

"Mom's in New York with my dad, but Nadia might come." Nick turns fully toward me. "She's been warned that if she so much as blinks at you wrong she's gone."

I sigh because I don't want to stand between him and his family. "I'm sorry."

Nick leans down and kisses my forehead. "Don't

be sorry. Now let's get my baby some food."

He leads the three of us farther into the main room and over to the bar, and we order drinks. I'm sipping my boring ass club soda with lime when Heidi and Greta show up.

Greta is our bohemian princess, and her long, flowy dress reflects that. Her brown hair hangs down her back in beautiful waves. Heidi has her hot pink tipped blonde hair in a bun on top of her head. She's in black tuxedo wide leg pants that sit low on her narrow hips. She's wearing a silvery top that molds to her body, and it shows a sliver of skin. Both of my baby sisters are a couple of beauties. They wave at us as we approach. We give kisses and then ask Joaquin to take our pictures.

Nick takes me around, introducing me to coaches and players. I didn't realize that on the off season a lot of the players work full-time jobs because arena football players don't make a lot.

When he leads me back toward my family, I see that Victoria and Miles are here. We ask one of the players to take a picture of all of us together. With our arms around each other we smile for the camera. The picture looks great, so maybe I'll frame it for everyone.

Nick looks off to the side. "Our new quarterback is here. I have to talk to him before we talk to the press. Colton, over here brother."

It's like a car crash because Colton walks toward us, and I immediately know who that is—the man who broke my baby sister's heart. He sees all of us as he approaches. His face immediately pales, and when he claps eyes on Heidi I can only describe the look as one of love and pain.

I turn back to Heidi, and the look on her face makes me want to cry. The pain rolls off of her in waves.

"Heidi," he whispers, not even trying to hide the pain in his voice. Colton approaches her slowly. Not even thinking, all of us Collins siblings close in on Heidi, acting as protection. "Can we talk?"

Miles steps forward, but Heidi stops him. "I have nothing to say to you." She steps back and then quickly walks out of the room.

Colton goes after her. I turn to look at my sisters, and they all wear worried looks on their faces. "Should one of us go after them?" Miles asks.

"What's going on? How does Heidi know our new QB?" Nick looks at all of us with confusion on his face.

I grab his hand, and we walk to an empty corner. "They started dating in junior high. At first it was just sweet puppy love, and by the time they hit high school they were inseparable. When he left, he broke my sister. None of us knows what happened."

"He's an amazing quarterback, and we can't get rid of him."

I nod. "Of course. No one expects you to. I just wouldn't count on her being at a lot of games."

He kisses the back of my hand and leaves me with my family while he talks to the guy from one of the local news channels.

By the time the party winds down I'm beat. I try to hide my yawning from Nick, but he catches me. "Why don't you ride home with Mona and Joaquin? You're beat, and I'm going to be here for a while."

"Okay, I'll see you later." I tilt my head back, accepting his kiss. He says goodnight to Mona and Joaquin.

I'm surprised that Nick doesn't even offer to walk me down. I watch him walk to Gordo who has a couple of those girls standing with him. A sick feeling washes over me, but I push it away.

"Sierra, are you ready?" Mona pulls me from my thoughts. I take her hand, and she leads me to Joaquin. Before we head downstairs, I turn around and take one last look at Nick.

He sees me and gives me a smile and a chin lift. I wave, and then we take our leave. I'm not an insecure woman, and he's never given me any inclination that he's a cheater. Nick has shown me how devoted he is to me and this baby.

They drop me off at Nick's, and once I'm inside the apartment I head into his bedroom. I get undressed and then in the bathroom, I brush out my hair and then pile it up on top of my head before washing my face and brushing my teeth.

I strip out of my bra and panties, climbing into bed, and burrow under the covers, falling asleep almost instantly.

I'm working on a sketch for a client, and my mind keeps drifting to the night before. Nick woke me when he got home with his mouth between my legs. After I came, he eased up my body and entered me slowly.

He made love to me slowly until we came

together, and then we fell asleep with my back snug against his front.

"Sierra?" I turn with a start and find Greta beside me. "Where were you with that dreamy look on your face? Did Nick give you the goods last night?" The brat does a humping motion, and I swat at her.

"Don't you have work to do?" Saturday's are our busiest days. We have it worked out that Mona starts her clients at nine, and the rest of us take turns closing.

I'm sure once the baby comes I'll be adjusting my hours, but hopefully by then Lainey will be tattooing, and we won't have to worry about losing business.

Tonight, Heidi and I are closing, and I'm hoping to have the chance to talk to her about Colton. She never came back to the party, but he did—looking miserable most of the time. I wanted to talk to him, but Joaquin stopped me. He told me it wasn't our place to get involved unless either of them came to us.

Joaquin was right; it wasn't our place to get involved. That doesn't mean I'm not going to ask my sister what's going on.

"You're so bossy." She sticks her tongue out at me and grabs her next appointment, bringing him back to her workstation.

As soon as I finish my sketch, I text my appointment and let her know I'm ready for her to come back. While I wait, I grab myself a ginger ale and pour it into my cup.

A few minutes later my appointment shows up,

and I get to work.

When it's finally time to close up, I lock the front door. I find Heidi sitting at the desk in the office. "What are you doing?"

She looks up at me and smiles, but I don't like what I see in her eyes—sadness fills them, and she's doing a crappy job trying to hide that. "I'm just uploading pictures onto all of our social media accounts." Heidi looks me over. "How are you feeling? I've noticed you haven't been as sick."

"I'm feeling better. We found lots of tricks to keep me from getting sick.." I sit across from her. "What's up with Colton?"

Heidi's body stiffens, and she keeps her eyes on the laptop. "Nothing's up."

"That didn't seem like nothing."

"We dated. We broke up—the end." She continues typing on the keyboard.

I lean forward. "Honey, we all thought you guys were going to be together forever."

She looks up at me. "So did I." I open my mouth to respond, but she stops me. "I don't need or want the advice of someone who got knocked up by her fuck buddy." My body jerks like it's been hit.

Heidi grabs her bag and storms out of the office. Once the shock of her words wear off, I jump up and chase after her, but she's already out the door, in her car, and pulling out of the parking lot.

I lock the door and head back to the office and grab my phone. Shooting Heidi a quick text, I hope she reads it.

Sierra: I'm sorry. I shouldn't have pried. You both just looked so sad. I love you, Heidi Ho.

I stare at my phone, waiting for the black dots to start bouncing, but after twenty minutes I'm convinced she's not speaking to me now. I quickly pull up Greta's number since they're roommates and call her.

"Hey, sis, what's up?"

I quickly tell her about Heidi. "I feel bad and should've kept my mouth shut."

"That may be, but she doesn't have the right to talk to you like that."

"Greta, she didn't mean it. She was lashing out because she's upset. Heidi used to do that a lot when we were younger."

"True, but she should apologize."

Greta and Miles have always been the peacekeepers in the family. "Just keep an eye on her, and don't lecture her." I'm quiet for a second and then ask, "Do you know what happened between them?"

"Not really, and it was so sudden. It was like he just vanished. You were going to school and trying to help Mona with Iris. Heidi was a robot after that for a while. I honest—oh shit, I hear her keys in the door. I'll talk to you later. Love you, bye!"

I sweep the floor and then stock my station. I take a quick lap through the studio, shutting off lights. I don't relish the idea of walking out to my car alone, but I've got pepper spray.

I set the alarm and get my keys out of my bag. I step outside and quickly lock the door. I turn around to hustle to my car and find Nick leaning against it, looking sexy as fuck in jeans and a blue sweater that shows off his muscular build.

"What are you doing here?"

He holds out his hand to me, and I take it, letting him pull me into his arms. "Greta called Mona, who told Joaquin, who then told me that Heidi left you alone to lock up."

I shake my head. "It's seriously not a big deal. She was upset and needed to leave. As you can see, I'm okay," I say, holding my free hand out.

He pulls me close and puts his big palm over my barely there baby bump, and I won't lie, my heart races, and butterflies take flight in my belly. "That may be, but you've got precious cargo here, and I need both of you to always be safe."

I look up at him. "You can't say stuff like that to me while I'm pregnant. I'm prone to bouts of crying. Plus, who are you? Where's the guy who says inappropriate things and says them loudly?"

"Oh, he's still here. How about we head back to my place, and I'll suck on your tits while you ride my cock?"

My face heats up. "Ugh... I should've kept my mouth shut." I poke him in the chest. "If my baby's first word is tits, I'm seriously going to kick your ass."

We head back to his place, leaving my car at the studio. It's late and when we get back I change into my jammies and head into the bathroom to wash my face and brush my teeth.

With my toothbrush in my mouth, I look at myself in the mirror. I run a hand over my slight baby bump and then turn to the side, pulling my t-shirt up. I look extremely bloated more than anything.

I spot Nick in the doorway watching me with a

heated gaze, and his blue eyes just pop. "You take my fucking breath away. I may have to keep you knocked up for as long as I can."

"Let's see how we do with this one first," I tell him after I spit my toothpaste out. I walk toward him and stop inches away. "It's so weird to think about the fact that there is a baby in here."

"Part of me and part of you, and I can't wait to meet him."

I shake my head and between him, my dad, brother and Max they're all rooting for a boy. I honestly don't care; I just want a healthy, happy baby.

Nick scoops me up in his arms and carries me into his bedroom where he proceeds to do the dirty stuff that he spouted earlier, and I enjoy every fucking second.

EVAN GRACE

NICK

I'm beginning to put together the new menu at *Nicholas* when my office phone rings. I see it's the maître d's number. "Hi, Carol."

"Sorry to bother you, Mr. Echols, but your father's here. Should I send him back?"

My dad never stops by unannounced. If I had to guess, this is about the baby. I'm sure Mom or Nadia have told him. Honestly, I should've done it sooner, but there has been too much going on. "You can send him back."

Of course when my father arrives, he doesn't even knock—he just walks right in. I stand and extend my hand for him to shake. "Well, this is surprise. For what do I owe the pleasure?"

"What's this I hear about you knocking up some tattoo artist? Your mother and sister are beside themselves."

I now know how Joaquin felt when the shit went

down with his dad and how he felt at first about Mona. Just like my brother, I'm not letting this go any further. I lean in, lowering my voice. "She's not just some tattoo artist. All you need to know is that I'm falling in love with her, and we're starting a family."

"You're making a mistake." He leans in. "Give her some money and have her take care of this."

Immediately I see red and advance on him until he hits the door. "Are you kidding me? That is your grandchild."

"Nicholas, stop being so dramatic. It was just a suggestion." He straightens his suit jacket. "Call your mother and let's set up a dinner so we can all get to know *her*." God, he's a dick. I'm not sure I want to subject Sierra to my family again.

"How's business?" Leave it to my father to go from one topic to another. "You have a full house out there already today."

"Of course I do. Our food is phenomenal." We'll be opening our reservation books soon and will be booked up in less than twenty-four hours. At *Blaze*, we've started to use the upper floor for events.

He turns and grabs the doorknob then looks at me over his shoulder. "Call your mother."

And with those parting words he's gone. God forbid he tell me he's proud of me. I shake it off and meet with my executive chef. We set up a time for me to show him the upcoming menu and have him taste the selections.

I save the menu and grab my bag. On the way out to my car I send Joaquin a text, asking if he wants to meet for a beer. He tells me that Mona's at the studio, but to come over and have a beer with him.

94

As soon as I pull into the driveway, Iris, Max, and Fluffy come running out to greet me.

"Uncle Nick," they call in unison as they run to me.

I scoop up Iris into my arms and the littlest Collins female kisses my cheek and wraps her arms around my neck. Max is too cool for a hug, so we fist bump. I kiss Iris' cheek before setting her down.

Joaquin meets me at the front door. "Hey, what's up, brother?"

We exchange backslapping hugs. "My father showed up at *Nicholas* today so he could share his opinion about Sierra." I follow him into his kitchen where he grabs me a beer. "How did you and I get to be so awesome, even with asshole dads?"

"Maybe we were adopted." Joaquin holds up his beer, and we clink our bottles together.

"You're all coming to the season opener, right? You guys get to sit in the owner's suite with us. Gordo's got jerseys for both of the kids."

Joaquin looks outside to where the kids are running around with the dog, and I don't miss the smile on his face. He turns back to me. "Yeah, we'll be there. The girls are closing the studio early so they can all come."

"Fantastic. I'm so fucking stoked. A couple of these guys could get picked up by the NFL. I have a feeling that Colton is going to get signed by the end of the season."

"Mona said when he played in high school he was phenomenal." Joaquin takes a drink of his beer. "How are things with you and Sierra?"

"Good, I'm just biding my time until I start

pushing for more. I want my ring on her finger before the baby comes, but I have a feeling it's going to be hard to persuade her to let that happen. We're practically living together. More of her stuff keeps ending up at my place, which is exactly what I want." I'm not sure if she notices it or not, but I love seeing her shit hanging in my closet and in my drawers.

Mona comes in while I'm finishing my beer. I watch as she goes right to Joaquin, wrapping her arms around his waist. He kisses her and then looks at her in a way that makes me extremely happy for my friend.

She comes toward me and gives me a squeeze before heading out the back door to greet the kids. I watch as she hugs and kisses them both. "You're a lucky motherfucker. I hope you know that." Max's mom hardly ever sees him, and she barely acknowledges she has a kid.

Joaquin sighs happily. "Trust me, I know. She treats him like she pushed him out of her body and loves him fiercely already."

"She's lucky too. You're the best dad to both of those kids, and that little girl has you wrapped so tightly around her little finger."

Joaquin shakes his head and laughs. "That she does. I can't wait to give them another brother or sister—hell, maybe a couple more."

Neither of us have big immediate families, and now he's thinking of expanding. If things go the way I want, Sierra and I are going to have a whole mess of beautiful blonde babies.

From our box, I look around the stadium and smile. It's our season opener tonight, and we're sold out. Attendance started dipping last year, and in order to keep that from happening we've tried to make it more fun for everyone to come.

Before the game, we had food trucks, face painters, clowns, and a local band playing. I glance over at Max and Iris—her whole face is a glittery butterfly, and Max looks like Spiderman.

Sierra and her sisters all have a butterfly on their cheeks. They're all sporting Atlanta Fire t-shirts, except the kids who are wearing jerseys. We've got our own private bartender and a spread of appetizers.

I feel arms wrap around me from behind and turn my head to see Sierra standing there. I pull her around to my front and wrap my arms around her waist, with a hand resting on her baby bump.

"Nick, this turnout is incredible. I don't know anything about sports, but the team is on fire. Colton is amazing." She says the last part quietly. I'm still not sure what happened because Sierra said that she doesn't really even know.

As long as it doesn't affect Colton's playing then I'm going to stay out of it.

When the final whistle blows, Atlanta Fire are ahead of Chicago Stars fourteen to seven. Gordo and I head down to the field to congratulate the coaches and the team.

The energy is electric as we step onto the field. Coach Stan and I share a backslapping hug.

"Congratulations, Coach. They played a helluva fucking game."

He thanks me, and then Gordo is congratulating him. I congratulate the players, and a reporter from Channel Five news stops me to get my comments on the game and what I think about our upcoming season.

"I think our offensive and defensive lines worked as well-oiled machine. The team is outstanding, if I do say so myself. I think we've got a great shot of the team going really far."

Colton walks up as I'm finishing up, and the reporter turns the camera on our QB. The guy is a natural. I can totally see the NFL snatching him up before the end of the season.

I spot my girl, her sisters, Joaquin and the kids standing on the sidelines. I wave them over, and they all come except Heidi who turns and hightails it toward the exit.

Colton must spot her because he takes off running after her. Sierra and her sisters watch him chase after her with the same worried looks on their faces.

"Mom, why was that football player chasing after Aunt Heidi?" Iris looks up at Mona.

She looks down at her daughter. "They used to be boyfriend and girlfriend."

I don't hear the rest of their conversation because I head toward Sierra. She jumps into my arms. "Congratulations on the win." Her smile is blinding.

Leaning down, I kiss her thoroughly until I hear catcalls by her sisters and Joaquin. I pull back and set

Sierra gently on her feet. "Everyone is heading to Club after this to celebrate. Do you want to come?"

Sierra yawns, covering her mouth with the back of her hand. "I'm so tired. Would you be mad if I went home?"

I shake my head. "No, baby. Are you going to my place or yours?"

"Mine. I need to clean and do some laundry before I go to the studio tomorrow. You have keys, so you can come to my place when you're done." She kisses me one more time before she goes to her sisters. Greta is giving her a ride home.

Joaquin gives me a backslapping hug. "Thanks for having us, brother. This was a whole lot of fun. The kids had a blast."

"Anything for you, man, you know that. I love you, brother." I hug him again before letting him go. After hugs and kisses to the rest of the clan, they all take off.

Gordo comes running over. "Are you ready to hit Club?" I nod, and we head up to the owner's box to grab our stuff before we head out.

EVAN GRACE

SIERRA

I lie on my side and watch the way the shadows dance across the wall. This has been the day from hell, and I wish I could just fall asleep so it will be tomorrow and maybe it'll be a better day.

Why was it a bad day, you ask? Well, let's rewind, and I'll tell you.

When I got home last night, I was exhausted, and in no time I was fast asleep. When I woke up, my morning sickness was bad, and I spent quite a bit of time hunched over my toilet.

After my stomach settled down, I grabbed some ginger ale out of the refrigerator and then hopped into the shower. When I got out, I walked into my bedroom and frowned at my empty bed.

I thought for sure that Nick was going to come over last night, but he never did. I picked up my phone and didn't see any text messages from him. He probably had too much to drink and went home and passed out.

In my bra and panties, I went back into the bathroom and sprayed some detangler in my hair and then combed it through. I quickly dried it and threw it up in a top knot because I didn't feel like doing anything with it.

I applied a little makeup, not going whole hog because I just felt blah. My boobs hurt, and I was so freaking tired. I slipped on some black and white checkered leggings, black leg warmers, because why not, an off-the-shoulder purple long-sleeve t-shirt, and my matching purple Chucks.

Honestly, I looked ridiculous, but I was so comfortable I didn't care. While I made myself some toast, I grabbed my phone and started thumbing through Instagram.

I hit the like button on a picture of Greta. It was her profile with the sun setting behind her. Fuck, my sister is such a beauty—if I didn't love her so much, I'd be totally jealous.

A picture on the Atlanta Fire's page caused me to pause. It was a couple of players, but in the background was Nick and a redhead with their arms around each other that grabbed my attention.

She was tagged in the photo, and like an idiot I clicked on it and her profile came up. There was a picture of the two of them, and her caption made my stomach turn.

This is the best guy right here. Super lucky to be spending the evening with him. #Luckygirl #Night2Remember

I ran to the bathroom and made it to the toilet just as my stomach bile came up because, of course, my stomach was empty. I wiped my mouth off and re-brushed my teeth.

I wasn't going to jump to conclusions even though he didn't come to me last night. Nick wasn't Lance.

When I got to the studio, Mona was there, and she grabbed me as soon as I came through the door. Once we crossed the threshold, I spotted my other sisters on the loveseat.

"What's going on? Is this an intervention?" I laughed nervously

Mona took a seat on the arm of the chair I was sitting on. "We saw the Instagram post. We saw her post, honey." She grabbed my hand. "Have you talked to him?"

I shook my head. "I saw it too, but I'm not going to freak out. If I can't trust him then we shouldn't try this dating thing."

"Okay, sis." They looked at me skeptically but all took their leave.

Heidi stopped and turned back to me, pulling me into a hug. "I'm sorry what I said to you. You didn't deserve that." She kissed my cheek and then went out front.

I had back-to-back clients which thankfully kept me occupied the rest of the night, but now that I'm home and in bed alone with my thoughts, I'm freaking out. I only heard from Nick once today, and that was to tell me he was hungover and going to take a nap and then take his sister out for dinner.

Now in the quiet of my apartment my mind is pulling up every bad scenario in my head. This time when the incident with Lance pops into my head it's

Nick and the redhead.

My stomach turns, but I breathe deep and try to ignore the pain in my chest. I close my eyes and try to think of anything other than Nick. The only thing that gets me to a point I can feel myself start to get it tired is the image of the little baby growing inside of me.

I open my eyes and notice something is off. I feel a lot of heat at my back, and there is a very large hand covering my belly.

I try to scooch away from him, but he pulls me until I'm snug against his body. "I know you saw the posts. I'm so fucking sorry, baby. The one on the Fire's page was from when she got there and congratulated me on the team's win. The other one was her asking to get a picture with me." Nick kisses the back of my head. "I would not do that to you."

Everything inside me says to believe him, but there's a very small part of me that thinks he's lying. Maybe something hasn't happened yet, but what if it does? I push the bad thoughts away.

Nick brushes my hair off of my neck and places a kiss behind my ear while I brush my teeth. "What do you have planned today?" he asks with his lips against my neck.

I spit and rinse. "Nothing really." He grabs my towel and wipes my mouth off. "What about you?"

"I'd like to take my girl out to breakfast, go back to my place, and cuddle all day. That way we can head to your OB appointment in the morning from my place."

On that thought I smile. I get to hear my baby's heartbeat tomorrow. I turn and smile up at his handsome stupid face. "That sounds good."

I throw on some bootcut jeans, but when I go to button them but I can't. I try sucking it in, but it doesn't help. With a growl I pull them off and throw them across the room—almost hitting Nick who is standing in my doorway.

"Is there a problem?" He smirks, and I just want to punch him.

"My jeans won't button." I pull up my white sweater with hot pink skull and crossbones so my stomach is exposed. "I'm getting fat," I say with a huff.

Nick comes toward me, a predatory look on his face. "I don't want to hear you ever say that you're fat. You're beautiful, and you're cooking our baby." He places his hand on my baby bump. "Get on the bed, baby?"

His voice is thick with desire, and I do what he says, lying back, and I watch as he climbs on the end of the bed. Nick grabs my ankles and pulls my legs apart. "I-I thought we were going to breakfast?" As he crawls between my legs, I begin to pant.

"Oh I'm gonna eat." Nick bends down and pulls the gusset of my panties aside and swipes his tongue up and down my pussy. He moans as he begins to fuck me with his tongue.

"Oh God, Nick. You're so good at this." I feel him push one finger, then two, inside me. My hands go to his head as he rubs my G-spot. I come almost immediately, giving a surprised cry.

Nick brings me down slowly and when he pulls

out his fingers, he licks them clean. "Fuck me, but you taste sweet."

He pushes up and moves until we're face to face. Nick nuzzles my neck and causes goose bumps to pop up all over my body. His stubble tickles me, and I giggle like a silly schoolgirl.

My stomach growls loudly, causing us both to laugh. "Let's get you fed, baby … and, baby." He maneuvers his body down mine until his lips hover over my lower abdomen as he places a kiss there. "Daddy's going to feed mommy, and I love you."

My eyes begin to burn, and a lump forms in my throat. I close my eyes so he can't see the tears threatening to spill. He helps me off the bed, and I throw on a pair of leopard print leggings and a pair of black ballet flats.

The whole time I finish dressing I force the thoughts of him cheating on me from my mind.

I stare at the time on my phone and then look toward the door. Nick is late—this morning his manager at *Blaze* called with a problem, so after breakfast Nick got dressed in his sexy, sleek navy-blue suit, crisp white dress shirt unbuttoned at the collar, and a red pocket square, then left.

The nurse calls my name, and I look at the door one more time. I sigh as I stand and follow the nurse into the back. She weighs me and tells me I've lost almost ten pounds since my last appointment.

She has me stop by the bathroom to give a urine sample. I wash my hands and step out of the restroom, and she takes me to an exam room. She takes my vitals she then helps me lie back. She pulls my bottoms down to my pubic bone.

A knock on the door has her answering it. Nick comes walking through the door. "I didn't miss the heartbeat, did I?" He stops next to me and leans down, kissing my lips.

"No, she was just getting ready to do it."

Nick takes a seat by my head and grabs my hand in both of his.

The nurse squirts a dollop of gel on my stomach and places a little microphone on my belly. My hand trembles in Nick's as the nurse moves it around, pressing on different spots. All of a sudden a fast whooshing sound fills the room.

"Here's your baby's heartbeat," she announces. "One hundred and fifty-five beats per minute."

"That's good?" Nick asks her.

"It is." She lets us listen for a few more seconds before she takes it off and hands me some paper towels. "Dr. Honn will be in, in a few minutes."

The nurse leaves, and I turn to look at Nick, who is grinning from ear to ear. "Was that not the sweetest sound in the whole wide world?"

"It sure was, baby. I'm sorry I was late. The refrigerator was acting up and was starting to freeze stuff. I had to make sure the repairman got there sooner rather than later, and it cost a lot of cake to get it fixed right away."

"Was any food ruined?" I know he's said that they use fresh ingredients, but they have to store everything somewhere.

Dr. Honn interrupts us, and after I introduce her

to Nick, she does her examination. "Well, everything looks good. I don't like the weight loss, but that can happen with morning sickness. You're measuring right on track."

She types some stuff into her computer and then looks up at me. "We'll see you in four weeks. At that appointment we'll schedule your ultrasound and, hopefully, if you guys want, you can find out the sex of the baby."

We head out to the front, and I schedule my next appointment. In the waiting room I don't miss the way all the women openly gawk at Nick. He stops to look at the newborn baby in his or her mother's arm.

He smiles at me and grabs my hand, leading me out of the office. When we reach the lobby, Nick lets go of my hand and wraps his arm around my shoulders.

"You didn't get a chance to finish telling me, but did anything get ruined?"

He shakes his head. "No, luckily Matthew came in early and caught it. It's a downside when you own your own restaurant. Do you have to get to the studio?"

"Yeah, I have an appointment at one. Mona asked me to babysit tonight." I love spending time with those kids. "Their babysitter cancelled on them. She called when I was on my way here."

"Okay, I'm heading back to *Blaze* to take care of some stuff and then head to *Urban Fusion*. I haven't been there in over a week. How about we take your car back to my place. I'll take you to the studio, and then I'll take you to Joaq and Mona's?"

"Sure."

Like a true gentleman he walks me to my car. He wraps me in his arms as we reach it and proceeds to kiss me until my toes curl, and I tingle between my legs.

Nick waits until I pull out of the spot before he walks in the direction of his car.

EVAN GRACE

NICK

"Faster, Uncle Nick." Iris giggles herself silly as I do pushups with her sitting on my back.

Sierra watches from the sofa with Fluffy in her lap. God I love her, and I'm afraid to tell her because I'm worried that it would scare her off. Things have been good between us, even after the Staci episode.

Fuck, I was so pissed when I saw those posts. I'm not sure what her game is, but I don't like it. I haven't really had a chance to think about how I'm going to handle it, but I need to do something.

I focus back on my pushups and feel Iris lay down so we're back to back. Her long hair tickles my neck, and she shouts for her aunt to take a picture of us. I freeze mid pushup, let Iris roll to her side, and we both say cheese as we smile for the camera.

Iris gets off, and I roll to my back, grabbing Max. He knows the drill, so he crosses his arms over his chest and holds himself stiff as I begin bench pressing him.

An hour later, we're done tucking the kids in. Sierra and I head downstairs, and she curls up next to me as I cross my legs at the ankles on the coffee table.

It isn't long before I feel Sierra go lax beside me. Joaquin and Mona both said the fatigue will get better once she gets through the first trimester, which is only about a week away.

I stroke her hair as I think about the sweet sound of our baby's heartbeat inside of her. It just makes it that much more real. I hug Sierra to my side and kiss the top of her head.

Joaquin and Mona come home about an hour later. Those two are so blissfully happy, and I want that with Sierra and our baby. We say our goodbyes, and I take my girl home and go about showing her with my body that I love her. I hope that she gets the message.

Sierra's knee bounces nervously from the passenger seat as we pull onto the long and winding driveway that leads to my parents' home. We're having dinner with them and Nadia.

My sister has been warned that if she so much as looks at Sierra the wrong way we're going to have words. Nadia promised she'd behave, but I'm not going to hold my breath on that one.

I pull up my car in front of the giant white monstrosity I grew up in. My father has always had to have the best of everything so he could prove how great he was to his peers and how he has the best of everything.

"Wow, this is where you grew up?" Sierra leans forward to look up at the house from the front windshield. "I grew up in a nice home, but ours could've fit into this one about five times over."

I climb out and come around to her side, helping her out of the car. The front door opens, and my mom appears in the doorway. "There's my handsome boy."

Letting go of Sierra, I wrap my arms around my mother and hug her tight. "Hi, Mom. You remember Sierra."

Thankfully she pulls Sierra into a hug. "Darlin', you look beautiful. How are you feeling?"

"I'm starting to feel a lot better, but exhausted all of the time."

Mom loops her arm through Sierra's and leads her toward our sitting room. "Feeling tired will come and go throughout your pregnancy, but I guess that's your body's way of preparing you for getting no sleep with a newborn."

In the sitting room we find my father and sister talking quietly, both with drinks in their hands. They stand, and I hug my sister and kiss her cheek. I shake hands with my father and then grab Sierra's hand. "Dad, this is Sierra Collins. Sierra, this is my father, Burton."

"It's nice to meet you, Mr. Echols." Sierra holds out her hand, and he takes it, thankfully keeping any rude comments to himself. "Hi, Nadia."

"Sierra." My sister's tone is bored, and I'd love to bop her on the head for acting like a stuck-up snob.

"Nicholas, Sierra, have a seat. What can I get

you to drink, Sierra? Scotch and soda for you, Nick?"
My mother has always been the perfect hostess.

"I'll just have water please."

I sit next to Sierra, and my mother hands me my
drink. "Thanks, Mom. I have something for you guys
to hear." I pull out my phone and pull up the sound
recording of our baby's heartbeat. I press play and
hold it up. "Our baby's heartbeat."

I know I'm smiling like a lunatic, but I don't
care because that's the most beautiful sound I've ever
heard. I look at my family; Mom's smiling with
bright eyes, my father looks bored—typical—and my
sister's face is unreadable.

"How wonderful. Burton, isn't this great. A little
grandbaby to spoil and love." She claps her hands
together. I can tell she's faking it, but I appreciate the
pretend enthusiasm. It's not that she's not happy. I
just know she'd feel better if Sierra and I were
married.

"It was so amazing. I couldn't believe how fast
it was, but she said it was totally normal. At my next
appointment they'll be scheduling the ultrasound, and
we get to find out the sex of the baby," Sierra says.
Her lips are tipped up in a gorgeous smile.

"Nicholas, that was a helluva game the Fire
played. I still don't understand why you felt you
needed to become co-owner of an arena football team
when you've got three very profitable restaurants. If
you were looking for investment opportunities, I
could've helped you with that." Leave it to my dad to
give me backhanded compliments and completely
blow off everything that Sierra said.

"I saw the picture of you and the cheerleader on

Instagram," Nadia says, and I don't miss the way Sierra stiffens next to me. "You seemed awfully cozy. Where were you Sierra?"

"Ahem... I was at home." She shifts next to me uncomfortably.

I'm so pissed right now. I stand. "Nadia get up." My sister shoots Sierra a snooty grin and gets up, letting me lead her to the hallway. "What the fuck did I tell you?" I growl.

"Oh come on, I was just trying to get a rise out of her. I didn't mean any harm."

"Really? Because I think you're just trying to be a bitch." I ignore her gasp. "I love you, you know I do, but this needs to fucking stop."

Nadia sighs. "Fine. I'll try to be nice to her."

"Nick?" I turn to find Sierra standing behind us. "I'm not feeling well. Can you please take me home?"

Pulling her into my arms, I hug her close. "Is it the baby?"

"I don't think so. I just don't feel well."

"This dinner is over. Mom, we're leaving," I call out, and I don't bother waiting for any of them to reply. Sierra and our baby are my priority.

I lead her outside to my car and help her inside. Climbing in the driver's side, I start my car, and we pull out and head back to my place. She's silent on the drive, but once we're back at my place and she seems more comfortable with the setting, I start the conversation.

"What happened when I left the room?" I'm almost afraid what her answer is going to be. It gives me flashbacks to when Mona overheard Joaquin's dad talking about her, and because of that he almost lost her.

She shakes her head and sighs. "It wasn't bad. I mean, your dad did ask if I was sure the baby was yours and did I do it intentionally." I can feel the anger flaring up inside me. Sierra places her hands on my chest. "I'm not offended ... seriously. I know you're well off, and to a gold digger you're the perfect candidate for a baby daddy scheme. He's just looking out for you."

I cup her face with my hands. "Okay, baby. If it wasn't what he said then why did you want to leave?"

"Because I don't feel good; that's it. Sometimes I get migraines, and honestly it's been a while since I've had one. Don't you remember I was going to go to New York with you, but I got a migraine."

I nod because I remember that. A buddy from culinary school was opening a new restaurant, and he invited me and a plus one to come. I ended up taking Joaquin because Sierra had been in bed with a bad headache.

Scooping her up in my arms, I ignore her protests and carry her directly into my room. I lay her on top of my gray comforter and cover her with this gorgeous cream colored cashmere blanket that my sister bought me.

I close the blinds and draw the curtains until my bedroom is bathed in darkness. Sitting on the end of the bed, I grab her hand in mine. "What can I do for you, baby?"

"Umm ... just some water and Tylenol. I can't take my normal meds, but that stuff should help, and the headache isn't a full blown migraine yet."

I excuse myself and get what my girl needs to feel better. I also grab an ice pack and towel and carry everything into the room. She takes the pills and lets me lay the icepack on her forehead.

"Do you want me to lay with you?" I stroke her hair back from her face. "I will."

Sierra shakes her head. "No, I know you have a game tonight. Just have fun, and go Fire," she says in a cheerleader voice.

"Okay, but as soon as the game's over I'm coming back to you." I kiss her head.

As soon as I step out of the room guilt for leaving already consumes me. How am I going to be able to leave both of them … ever?

EVAN GRACE

SIERRA

I step inside Starbucks and scan the inside until I spot Nadia sitting at a table in the corner. Inviting her to meet for coffee had been my idea, but Nick wouldn't give me her phone number at first. He thinks the migraine I had last Sunday was triggered by his family and their behavior.

Nick finally did give it to me when I told him I just wanted her to get to know me for him and our child. I sent a text first, asking if I could call her. When she said yes, I did.

Our call lasted about sixty seconds—long enough for me to ask her to meet for coffee so we could talk and for Nadia to say yes.

As I approach the table I take her in. Her hair is the same color as Nick's and hangs over one slender shoulder. She's tall for a woman, with the body you'd find on a ballerina. Nadia's truly breathtaking; too bad her attitude sucks.

"Hi, Nadia, thanks for meeting me. I'm going to get a drink; do you want something?"

"Sure, I'll take an iced coffee with Splenda."

I grab our drinks and then join her back at the table. She actually thanks me for the drink, and I sit across from her. "I'm glad you agreed to meet me. I just wanted you to get to know me."

My stomach cramps a little, causing me to shift in my seat. I've had them all morning, and when I called the doctor she had mentioned that as my uterus grows cramping could happen. It's only when accompanied by bleeding that there's a problem.

I take a drink of my herbal tea. "I know you all think I got pregnant on purpose, but I swear I didn't. I'm not sure what more I can say, but this baby is a part of you too, whether you want it or not."

She takes a drink of her iced coffee. "Yeah, okay."

We sit in an awkward silence while we drink. Since she's not going to share any info on her own, I guess I'm going to just have to ask. "What do you do for a living?"

"I'm a party planner."

I'm not at all surprised that's what Nadia does for a living. Ugh ... I shouldn't think that; it's too judgmental. "Do you like it?"

"I do. In college I was always in charge of throwing the parties for my sorority. Now, most of my sisters hire me for any kind of party that they throw." She takes a drink and then looks up at me. "Plus I get paid really well to spend someone else's money."

We make small talk while we sip our drinks. I

shift again and place a hand on my stomach.

"Are you okay? You're pale." Nadia looks me over closely.

I shake my head. "I think I need to go to the hospital." Standing, I grab onto the table as I suddenly feel lightheaded. Nadia wraps her arm around my waist and leads me out to a white BMW sports car.

On the way to the hospital I call my doctor's office, and they tell me they're going to notify the ER that we're on our way. I close my eyes and pray that I'm not losing this baby. Yes, it wasn't planned, but this baby is so loved by both Nick and me already.

We pull into the parking lot at Piedmont and as we're walking inside I feel like I wet my pants. I look at Nadia, "I-I think I just lost the baby." I begin crying hysterically as she leads me inside and to the desk.

They get me into a wheelchair and register me quickly before I'm whisked into the back. Nadia says she'll be right back, and hopefully she's calling Nick. The nurse takes my vitals and then helps me get my bottoms off and covered in a sheet. I don't miss the bloody underwear and quickly look away.

She tells me she'll be right back. Nadia steps in a minute later. "Nick's on his way."

She prepares to walk out, but I stop her. "Please don't leave." Nadia nods, and sit down next to me, grabbing my hand in hers. "Thank you. I don't want to be alone."

The nurse comes back and starts an IV, telling me she's starting some saline. Someone comes in and takes my blood then they tell me that an ultrasound technician will be coming in to do an ultrasound.

I'm so happy when Dr. Honn walks in. "Hello, Sierra. I hear you've had cramping and bleeding. Obviously, it's worse than when you called the office earlier. We're going to figure out what's going on."

The tech comes in, and they get me in stirrups. They put a condom over the wand and then squirt some jelly on it. "Okay, Sierra, this is going to be a little uncomfortable."

Nadia holds tightly to my hand as they insert the wand inside me. I feel the pressure as the woman moves it around. She leans forward and presses a button. That beautiful whooshing sound fills the room, and I begin to cry.

She turns the screen toward me, and that's when I see my child. Dr. Honn smiles at me. "The baby looks perfect, Sierra. Here's the heartbeat." She points to the fast fluttering.

"Sierra!" I look toward the curtain as Nick comes in. Nadia gets up and moves so he can get close to me. He bends down kissing my forehead.

"Look at our baby," I tell him, and he turns toward the screen while Dr. Honn quickly tells him that the baby looks good.

The tech points at something on the screen, and they both look closely at it. "I think we found the culprit of your cramping and bleeding. You have a couple of small Subchorionic hematomas. It's a blood clot that's between the placenta and the uterus."

Well, that doesn't sound good, but she eases my mind. "There's no real cause, and for now I want you temporarily on bed rest. I want you to call the office and tell them to schedule you at the beginning of my day in a week, and we'll do another ultrasound to make sure there are no problems. I know bleeding is concerning, but I don't want you to worry. The baby looks amazing."

She finishes up and says goodbye to us. We thank her and the tech for everything, and the tech gives Nick the pictures of our baby.

"I'm gonna go, but I'm so glad you're okay." Nadia grabs my hand.

Nick bends down to kiss me again. "I'll be right back. I'm going to walk her out." While he's gone, the nurse comes in and brings me these God awful mesh-looking panties and a pad. "This will keep you protected until you get home." She helps me get them and my bottoms back on.

Nick comes back while the nurse is going over what bed rest means. She goes over the rest of the discharge papers and then brings a wheelchair in. Nick picks me up off the bed and gently places me in it.

All I know is I'm going to do whatever I have to do to protect my baby.

"Mona, if Nick doesn't stop hovering, my baby is going to be fatherless because I'm going to murder him," I whisper into the phone.

"Why are you whispering?" She laughs.

She can't see me, but I'm shaking my head. "Because I don't want to hurt his feelings. He's been so great, but he's driving me insane. We better get good news today because I don't think I'll survive another week of this."

"Honey, he's doing it for you and the baby. He loves you."

My heart stutters in my chest. "Does he?" Do I love him? I have strong feelings, but I'm not sure if it's love. The thought of loving him scares me.

"Oh God, how can you not see that he does. He'd move heaven and earth if you asked him to."

Warmth spreads through me because he would. Nick's been taking such amazing care of me. I hear footsteps and whisper, "He's coming. I've got to go. Love you."

"You're such a dork." Mona laughs and then hangs up.

Nick comes in carrying a vase of light pink tulips. Placing it on the end table, he plucks the card out of it. He smiles and looks up at me. "Nadia."

I guess her seeing me the way she did last week, scared and vulnerable, changed things. This is the second bouquet she's sent. Nadia also brought me a huge basket filled with bubble bath, bath salts, candles and lotions. She was so sweet, and I appreciate her trying.

"Everyone has been so sweet to me," I tell him from my spot on his sofa. "Hopefully everything is better, and I don't have to stay on bed rest anymore."

Nick comes over and sits beside me, wrapping his arm around my shoulders. "No matter what happens we'll deal." He reaches for me with his other hand and places it on my lower stomach. "I just want you and this little boy to be healthy and safe."

I rest my head on his shoulder. "Thank you for everything you've done for us." Mona's words play through my mind, but I don't dare say anything because if he tells me he loves me, I don't know what I'll do.

"Of course, baby. Are you ready to go?"

I nod, and he stands, pulling me with him. I'm surprised he doesn't try to pick me up and carry me out. Instead, he grabs my hand, lacing our fingers together.

The elevator opens and we step on, and a really gorgeous woman is standing inside. "Hey, Nick," she coos.

"Bridgette." He smiles and gives her a chin lift.

Did he sleep with her? Am I going to run into that a lot around here? I try not to think about it, but I don't miss that she's openly staring at him. I've never understood how women can do that. It's very clear we're together, but she doesn't care.

I roll my eyes and watch the numbers as we descend.

EVAN GRACE

NICK

I walk into my office that I share with Gordo at the stadium. I feel like I've been in a happy fog all day. Last week we got word that the hematoma that Sierra had dissolved. Her doctor wanted her to still take it easy, but she was no longer on bed rest.

She's tried to have sex with me a couple of times, and it's killed me to say no, but Dr. Honn said she wanted us to wait just a little while longer before we resumed sexual activity.

I've been jerking off on the regular, Sierra's also given me a couple of blow jobs, but she feels guilty every time. It's been absolute torture to have her wrapped around my body like a spider monkey or having her lips wrapped around my cock and not being able to reciprocate.

This morning she was in my shower, and I had come in to brush my teeth. She turned to the side, and I noticed that her baby bump was becoming more noticeable. I couldn't help but stare at it in awe; again, that my baby is growing inside of her.

We go back in two weeks, and if all is well we are good to go. Sierra is officially at the start of her second trimester, and I swear it's flying by. The best part is her morning sickness is gone.

It's been nice cooking for her again and busting out some of her favorites. I hope our child isn't a picky eater—if so, I'll get creative.

On the desk is a manila envelope with my name on it. It's the contracts Gordo had drawn up for some new vendors. I sit and go over them and then send a text to my lawyer to see if I can drop them off. Yes, my father is an attorney, but it's better for us if he doesn't handle my affairs.

I check the upcoming schedule and check to make sure the hotel rooms are booked for our first away game. Gordo knew when he asked me to be a partner that I couldn't do away games. My restaurants and Sierra are too important to me to be away from.

A knock on the door pulls my attention away from the computer. I find Staci standing in the doorway, wearing little bootie shorts and a sports bra meant to show off her rack.

That's why Sierra is so much sexier—she doesn't have to put all of her lady bits out there. She's sexy because of the way she carries herself, and that's all she fucking needs.

"Hey, Staci. What can I do for you?" I hate that I have to be nice to her, but I don't need for there to be problems.

She walks further into the office and leans against the desk. "Oh nothing. I just haven't seen you around much these past few weeks. I wanted to make sure you were okay."

"I'm fine. I just had some personal stuff that I needed to take care of." I shut down the computer and grab the envelope. "I've got to get going. I have a meeting at *Blaze*. I'll see you Sunday at the game."

I give her a friendly smile, walking past her and out of the office. Luckily she doesn't follow me out, but I have a feeling I'm going to have to keep an eye on her.

Staci wants to get her hooks in me, and she's the type of woman who will keep trying until she gets what she wants or until she destroys my relationship with Sierra.

I step inside my parents' home for dinner. Sierra opted to go have dinner at Mona and Joaquin's since last time she came here it didn't end well. I've noticed as this week has progressed that she's got more energy than she's recently had.

She's increased her hours at the studio, trying to make it up to the clients she had to reschedule. I'm worried she's going to push herself too hard, but Mona promised me she wouldn't let that happen.

I find my mom and Dad in the sitting room having cocktails. Mom smiles when I walk in. "Hi, honey. Can I get you a drink?"

"Yeah, thanks, Mom. I'll take a scotch and soda."

She stands and stops in front of me to kiss my cheek. I sit across from my father. "Where's Nadia?"

My father looks up from his phone. "She's overseeing some baby shower for one of her sorority sisters." He rolls his eyes because God forbid he be proud of the business she's started for herself.

Mom hands me my drink. "How's Sierra?"

"Better, thankfully."

"Have you asked her to take a paternity test yet?" My father looks up at me. "You protect your wealth, or she could go after it and try to take it all."

Sighing heavily, I just want this over so I can go. "Not gonna happen. She doesn't want my money, and it's my baby she's carrying. I'm not going to talk about this anymore."

"Burton, leave him alone." My mother to the rescue as always.

This dinner can't be over soon enough.

I pull into Mona and Joaquin's driveway a little after seven, glad the dinner with my parents is over. My father spent most of the time on a business call. At least my mother is good company ... most of the time.

I knock on the door before opening it. "Where's my baby momma?" I holler as I step inside.

"In the family room, baby daddy," Sierra answers back.

Fluffy, the white furball, comes to greet me, and I pick his wiggly butt up. He gives my neck a lick as I scratch him behind his ear. I find my woman and family lounging in the family room—both kids are lying on the floor in front of the fireplace.

"How was dinner?" Sierra asks as I sit next to her and wrap my arm around her shoulders.

I kiss her forehead. "It was dinner—same old, same old."

She rests her head on my shoulder and sighs. "I'm sorry."

"It's fine, babe, I promise."

We stay until the end of the movie the kids were watching and long enough to get hugs and kisses from Iris and a fist bump with Max. Mona says goodbye because she's heading upstairs to help the kids get ready for bed.

Joaquin walks us out. "I'll call you tomorrow," I tell him. He hugs Sierra goodbye, and we share our manly back slap hug. I help my girl into the car and then climb in.

"Did you guys have a good time tonight?" I ask as I grab Sierra's hand in mine, bringing it to my lips.

"We did. I helped make dinner and didn't throw up, so yay me. I made the meatballs for the spaghetti—you would've been proud."

As soon as we get back to my place, I get Sierra settled on the sofa and turn on the electric fireplace and grab the cashmere blanket she's claimed as her own. "Why don't you find us something to watch. I'm going to go change."

In my bedroom, I strip out of my dress shirt and slacks, setting them inside of my walk-in closet in the dry clean pile. I leave my white tank top on and throw on a pair of old, worn, comfy as hell flannel pants.

Back in the living room I find my girl curled up on the sofa with Netflix pulled up. "What are we watching?"

Sierra smiles at me over her shoulder. "Scream 4."

My girl certainly loves her slasher films. "Do you want something sweet to eat while we watch?"

"Is there any chocolate mousse leftover from last night?"

I bend down and kiss her lips. "Whipped cream on top?"

"Do you not know me at all? Of course I want whipped cream." Her smile is cheeky, and I kiss her one more time before I head into the kitchen and get my girl some chocolate mousse.

I slowly come awake moaning. It takes a second for the brain fog to clear, and that's when I realize that Sierra is between my legs and my cock is in her mouth.

Fuck, her mouth feels like heaven. My fingers sift through her hair, and I grip it close to her scalp as she deep throats me. "Fuck, my girl loves sucking my cock." Sierra moans around my—oh I'm going to say it—throbbing length, and I feel it all the way to my balls.

The desire to come hits me. "Baby, if you don't stop I'm going come in your mouth." That doesn't deter her because Sierra increases her suction and cups my balls in one hand.

My fingers tighten in her hair, and I groan as that heavenly feeling passes over me seconds before I come with a shout. Sierra swallows around my length, and a shudder sweeps over my body knowing that she is swallowing every drop.

Sierra licks the head of my cock, cleaning every bit of cum from it. She pushes up and smiles at me from between my legs.

"What was that for, baby?"

She shrugs and moves until she's straddling my lap. "I know you don't want to have sex until Dr. Honn gives us the okay, but I wanted to at least give you something. Plus, you've taken such good care of me."

I sit up and wrap my arms around her waist and nuzzle her neck. "Haven't you learned by now that I would do anything for you?"

Sierra wraps her arms around my neck and rests her cheek on the top of my head. An unknown amount of time passes before I move us to our sides. I snuggle up to her back, wrap my arm around her waist, and rest my hand on her barely there belly, falling into a contented sleep.

EVAN GRACE

SIERRA

A month has passed since the whole hematoma scare happened, and I'm sixteen weeks pregnant. I feel so good now, no nausea and no extreme fatigue. Two weeks ago Dr. Honn gave me the go ahead to resume all sexual activity, which would be great if my boyfriend would actually have sex with me.

Nick has rebuffed me every time I've tried to get me some. I get he's worried, and maybe I am too, but I'm also so freaking horny now that I can barely stand it. Sure, he's let me suck his dick because what guy is going to turn down a blow job, but I need to feel him inside of me.

Last night he was at *Nicholas* late, so I took advantage of being alone and was getting myself off in the middle of his bed when he came home. Unfortunately for me I was so into it that I didn't hear him come in until his door opened as I was coming.

He said nothing just stepped back out, slamming

the door behind him. Being hormonal meant I curled into a ball and cried until he came back in. Nick crawled into bed with me and pulled me into his arms. "I'm sorry, baby. That was an asshole move."

I didn't respond, just let him hold me until I fell asleep; although, I was still upset that he wouldn't touch me.

Now I'm at Phipps Plaza shopping for some maternity clothes. My baby bump is way noticeable now on my smaller frame. Lucky for me so far I've gained back the ten I lost with an additional ten, and I still look normal from behind.

I think the ten I've gained are in my tits because they're practically popping out of bras. I've noticed the veins in them are more pronounced—that must be why they're so sensitive. I swear I can orgasm from nipple play alone.

My sisters are all at the studio; otherwise, I'm sure they'd love to shop with me. I find two pairs of distressed jeans that have the wide band around the waist. The saleswoman said that they'll stretch to accommodate my growing belly.

I don't like any of the tops, so I head to my favorite store, Lucky Brand, and am thumbing through the t-shirts when I hear a woman talking behind me.

"Yes, girl. He's so hot." She pauses like she's listening to someone, and I know I shouldn't eavesdrop, but it's like she's talking right behind me. "No, we haven't had sex yet, but I know he wants to. He needs to break things off with the girl he's with now, but she's pregnant and he feels guilty."

Shit, whoever she's talking about, the poor

thing, doesn't have a clue that her world is about to get turned upside down.

The woman starts talking again. "Nick promised me he'd take care of this sooner rather than later."

My ears begin to ring and I pretend to examine the shirt in my hand. I turn to the side and see the woman behind me and I feel like I've been kicked in the gut. It's the redhead who's on the cheer/dance team for the Fire, the one who posted the picture of she and Nick like they were on a fucking date.

A rage I've never felt before comes over me. This bitch is trying to start some shit, and I'm not fucking having it. Nick has proven to me over and over that he's not Lance.

I walk right up to her and surprise the hell out of her. My guess is she wanted me to start crying so she could feel like she was driving a wedge between me and my man.

"I assume you're talking about my man since you've been trying to hang off his dick every chance you get."

She looks me up and down, and her lips curl into an evil fucking smile. "Of course I'm talking about Nick. You know he thinks you got pregnant on purpose. He told me that he's considering having you do the paternity test that his father wants. Enjoy your free ride, honey, because soon I'll be climbing on that ride, and I don't like to share."

She walks out of the store like she's walking the catwalk, and my heart pounds in my chest. With a trembling hand I hang the shirt up, pay for my purchases, and walk toward the exit. A strange fluttering sensation happens in my belly, and I freeze.

Dropping my bags at my feet, I put my hand on my belly and feel it again. It's faint, but it's there.

"Miss, are you okay?" I turn and spot one of the saleswomen walking up to me.

"Yeah, sorry. The baby moved for the first time, and it just surprised me." My voice cracks, and I'm ready to cry any second. I smile at her. "I promise these are happy tears."

"I have two little ones, and I remember what that feeling was like. Congratulations."

I thank her and head out into the mall. Luckily I don't see that redheaded bitch anywhere. All I know is no matter what happens with Nick and me, I've got this baby, who I promise to love with everything I have until the end of time.

"Sierra, this is perfect. I can't wait to see it when all of the shading is done." My client smiles at me as I put the clear adhesive over the outline of his huge arm piece. His next appointment is already booked, so he pays for his work today, leaving me a nice tip before heading out.

He was my last client, so I wipe down my station and my table really well before closing it down. I grab my phone and take it into the office and find Heidi sitting behind the desk, staring off into space.

We haven't really talked about Colton. It's obviously a subject that she does not want to discuss, and I respect that decision. I hope she knows I'm here for her if she needs me.

"Heidi?" She startles and turns toward me. "Honey, what is it?"

I come around the desk, squatting the best I can in front of her.

Heidi shakes her head. "Nothing, just thinking about stuff." She's wearing a V-neck t-shirt, and the tattoo we ALL tried to talk her out of peeks out from behind the material. Right over her heart are the words, *Love doesn't live here anymore.*

"I like what you've done with your hair." Her tips used to be hot pink and the rest of her hair was her natural blonde. Now all of her hair is dyed a cotton candy pink, and with her complexion it's stunning.

"Thanks. I went to Mona's girl. I just was ready for a change. Is your last appointment done?"

"Yeah, I was just coming in to upload the pictures onto the website and social media." She gets up so I can sit, but not before placing her hand on my little belly and smiling.

Once she disappears out of the office, I quickly upload the pictures and post them everywhere they need to go. Heidi comes back in with the cash from the register. We don't carry a lot of cash, so we keep it locked in our little safe, depositing it in the bank once a week.

I lock the office and head out front and find Heidi standing by the door waiting for me. We head out to our cars, and then I follow her out of the lot— she goes right, and I go left.

Nick and I talked after I went shopping, but I haven't told him about my run-in with Staci. Honestly, I don't know if I should. It could make things bad for him, and I'm sure he can't turn around and say he doesn't want to be an owner anymore.

Sure, he could fire her, but I don't know if she'd try to pull something with him. By the time I pull into my spot at Nick's, I decide for now I'm not going to say anything.

I don't see Nick's car when I climb out and grab my shopping bags out of the trunk. Carrying them inside, the concierge comes and opens the door to the elevators for me. "Thank you." I give him a smile.

When I reach the floor, I step off and let myself into his apartment. I take the bags into the bedroom and change into my pajamas; a pair of gray leggings and a black cami that can barely contain my new, big tits.

I wash my makeup off and brush out my hair before throwing it up into a knot on top of my head. In the kitchen, I grab some string cheese and grapes out of the refrigerator and get comfy on the couch.

It takes no time at all before I'm lost in the show *Workin' Moms* on Netflix. It's made me laugh and cry. I finish my snack and throw my trash away then lay on the sofa, watching the first episode of season two when I feel my eyes get tired.

I feel myself being lifted. "Hey, honey," I say as I snuggle into Nick.

"Shhh. Go back to sleep, baby." Nick lays me on the bed and pulls the blankets over me. "I'll be right back."

I fall back asleep, waking when I feel him slide into bed with me and pulling me into his arms.

"I felt the baby move today," I say quietly. Nick's hand immediately finds my belly. I put mine over his and squeeze it.

"What did it feel like?"

"Like butterflies in my stomach but in one spot. I put my hand on my stomach and swear I could feel it that way too." I roll over until we're face to face. "It was so amazing."

In the moonlight I can see him smile before he leans forward and kisses me. He tries to pull away, but I hold tight. "Make love to me, Nick. Please, I need you."

I do need him, and not just for sex. I can ignore the feelings swirling inside of me all I want, but they don't negate the fact that he's become so important to me.

What we're building is so much more than I was ever looking for. I can try to fight it all I want, but at the end of the day it's Nick, me, and our baby.

Nick's lips slam down on mine, and he rolls us so I'm straddling him. I whimper into his mouth as I come in contact with his cock. In seconds my panties are soaked.

He rolls us again, always mindful of my belly. Nick pulls off my cami and then my leggings and wet panties. "I should take my time, savor you, but I need to taste you so bad.

He dips his head and licks my pussy. My fingers immediately sift through his hair. Nick grabs me by my inner thighs and opens me more to his seeking tongue. I cry out as he licks circles around my clit and nips it with his teeth.

Slowly I feel him ease one finger inside me and suddenly I'm coming—hard. I'm making a mess, but Nick just groans, lapping it up and gently bringing me back down.

Call me a freak, but I pull him up toward me so I can taste myself on his lips. Nick loves when I lick his lips clean. I stop when I feel the head of his cock at my entrance and stroke his cheek with my thumb as he eases his big, beautiful dick inside of me.

"Fuck, you're so tight, hot, and wet," he whispers before kissing me and thrusting deep inside of me. "Beauty, pure fucking beauty." Nick pulls almost all the way out before easing back into me tortuously slow.

He holds himself up by his hands, avoiding touching my belly.

I grab his face. "You're not going to hurt me or the baby. I promise. I promise I'll tell you if you do."

He stares down at me. "Fuck!" Nick grounds out, grabs my thigh, and hikes it up over his hip. He lowers his body, and I swear he sinks further inside me.

Nick begins to fuck me faster and faster—the desire to come builds again. "I'm gonna come again," I whimper.

He reaches between us, rubbing my clit. "Play with your tits, baby. Help me get you there."

I reach up, pinching both of my nipples. I moan long and loud because they're so sensitive right now. Pair that with my heightened sex drive, and I feel myself clamp around him. I arch my neck as I come so hard my mouth opens with a wordless cry.

"Fuck, baby. You just got so hot and wet." Nick begins to pound into me, prolonging my orgasm so much so that I'm still coming when he starts.

He plants himself deep, and I can feel his cock

pulsing inside of me. We both catch our breath, and then he pulls out of me. "You okay?" Nick asks quietly.

I pull his face down to mine. "I'm great, but I do have to pee." I kiss his lips, and he rolls off of me. Climbing out of bed I walk in the nude into the bathroom and pray to myself that there is no blood.

I'm a little crampy, but Dr. Honn said that sex can cause that, but as long as it goes away there is nothing to worry about. I sit on the toilet, relieve myself, and when I wipe I look down. "Thank God," I whisper—no blood.

I flush then wash my hands and go back into the bedroom. Nick's got the sheet up to his waist and has his arms behind his head. "Everything okay?"

I climb into bed and cuddle up next to him. "Yep, everything is great."

Nick places his lips against my forehead. "I don't know about you, but I needed that."

I sigh. "I did too, baby." The fluttering sensation hits my belly, and I grab Nick's hand and place it on my stomach. "I just felt the baby move." Of course I don't feel the sensation again.

"Let me talk to him." Nick pushes me to my back, pulls the sheet back, and moves down the bed until he's hovering over my belly. "Son, this is your dad. I don't think it's really fair that you move for your momma and not for me. Don't worry because I still love you." He places a kiss there before he moves back up next to me.

As soon as he pulls me into his arms, I feel sleep pull me under.

SIERRA

I carry the tub of popcorn while Mona carries the drink carrier as we make our way back to the owner's box. Sure, we could've gotten drinks in there and they probably would've gotten snacks for us, but I needed out of there.

Nick and Gordo are entertaining some businessmen who have been complete assholes. They've been hitting on my sisters and me, even after Nick introduced me as his girlfriend. They must've missed the pregnant belly, or they just don't care.

Two of the guys, who wore wedding rings by the way, asked Nick and Gordo to introduce them to the cheerleaders afterward. One of them cornered Greta and had the nerve to ask her where else she was pierced.

She laughed it off and made her escape, telling me right away what happened. I told her I'd talk to Nick about it later. I didn't want to cause trouble, but

145

it was getting ridiculous.

I wish Joaquin would've come tonight. He would've handled it, I'm sure, but Iris wasn't feeling well, so he told Mona that she should come, and he'd stay with the kids. We decided to make it a Collins' sister night out—except Heidi didn't come.

We step inside and sit with Greta. "Anyone give you any trouble?" I ask as I hand her a soda.

"No." She looks behind us and then turns back to me. "You know I love Nick, but if he doesn't get these douche bags out of here I'm going to start kicking asses."

I look behind me and find Nick and the other men in a huddle looking at something on an iPad. The screen comes into view when one of them moves, and I notice that it's a scantily-clad woman. "Look at those tits." My eyes widen because it's Nick who's said it.

The pigs all start talking about her like she's a piece of meat. He looks up and catches me watching him, and he's got remorse written all over his face. I ignore it and turn around, listening to the sound of his big, dumb laugh.

Okay, it's not dumb, but he's pissed me off. This behavior is not the real him, it can't be. Of course when we first met that's exactly how he was, so maybe I shouldn't be surprised he's acting like this now.

My sisters and I cheer on the Fire to their victory. Colton is an amazing quarterback and so fun to watch, which makes me feel guilty because he broke my baby sister's heart. The team is undefeated right now, which is good for Nick and Gordo.

After the game, the men head down to the field while we stay up in the box. I rest a hand on my belly as I watch that redhead circle Nick like a Great White shark.

I open my mouth to tell my sisters about it, but shut it. Greta excuses herself and heads to the bathroom while I continue to watch Staci. I hate even admitting that I think she's beautiful, but she really is.

Staci looks like the type of woman who belongs on his arm. I watch as she approaches him. I notice immediately that the smile he's giving her is small and fake. Not the big beautiful one he gives me.

I turn to talk to Mona, but she appears to be watching the scene below. Her jaw clenches, and I put my hand on her arm. "What?"

"That redhead is constantly in Nick's face. Could she act anymore desperate?" Now normally we don't try to cut down members of the sisterhood, but we've both dealt with women like Staci.

The cheerleaders are all gathered around Nick, Gordo, and the creeps now that the players went into the locker rooms. I stand and ask, "Can you take me home?"

I can't watch them flirt with him anymore. I know he wouldn't do anything, but I don't think I can watch the other men he's with behave like that. I grab my phone out of my purse and pull up his name.

Sierra: I'm exhausted, so Mona's taking me home. I'll see you later.

Nick pulls his phone out of his pocket and reads it. He looks up toward us and holds up a finger. Greta comes back and places her hand on my bump, and I smile when she bends down and begins talking to the baby.

"This is your auntie Greta, and I'm going to be your favorite." She hugs me and Mona goodbye. I watch her step out of the room and disappear.

I look toward the field and don't see Nick anywhere, but I see Staci is looking at me. She looks away immediately, but I didn't miss the lip curl. This all seems very Lifetime movieish. Staci will try to come between us, and she'll almost succeed before she meets her untimely demise… Well, okay, that's a little morbid, but karma's a bitch, and so am I.

"When's your ultrasound?"

I smile because I've been waiting for this one. "Two weeks and yes, I want to know the sex of the baby. Do you think we should do one of those gender reveal parties?"

Mona starts clapping and hopping up and down. "Yes! Let me talk to Joaquin. We'll host it. We'll do it the Sunday after your ultrasound."

"Okay, thank you."

Nick walks in and comes toward me, pulling me into his arms. "I'm ready when you are."

The three of us make our way to the parking lot where Mona and Joaquin's Range Rover sits next to Nick's car. He's quiet, but does say goodbye to Mona. Once we're inside his car, he starts it up and pulls out behind my sister.

I want to ask him what's wrong, but I'm afraid of what his answer might be. We reach his place and silently make our way up to his apartment.

I head right to his bedroom, stripping out of my clothes and into my pajamas. In the bathroom, I take care of business, and I find Nick sitting on the end of his bed when I step into his bedroom.

He stops me from walking past him and pulls me until I'm standing between his legs. "I am not that guy," Nick says quietly.

"What?"

"I'm sorry about how I behaved tonight. I know they made you uncomfortable." Nick rakes his fingers through his hair. "Fuck me, I used act just like them except I didn't have a wife at home." He wraps his arms around my waist. "I would never, never do that to you. I would never disrespect you or what we have."

The conviction in his voice nails home that he means every word. I wrap my arms around his head, holding him to me. "I know you wouldn't. Those guys were big douche bags, Nick, and two of them had wives." I pull away far enough to tip his head back. "You've given me no reason not to trust you, but there's a tiny part of me that has trouble trusting men."

"Who broke your heart, baby?"

I crawl onto his lap the best I can. "I dated Lance all through college, and we were getting so serious that moving in together was discussed. Well, I surprised him one day at his apartment, and I caught him fucking his best friend. They'd been sleeping together as long as Lance and I had. The love of my life was gay, and I was his beard.

"I felt so stupid and foolish. Like who doesn't know that their boyfriend actually prefers penis. I will say that I wasn't mad about him being gay, but I *was* mad because he deceived me. He let me fall in love with him, give my heart to him, knowing that I wasn't what he really wanted." I take a deep breath. "He never apologized for doing it either. Last I heard was that they were married now and had a baby.

"After that I just swore I was never going to allow myself to fall in love. Easy breezy has been what I wanted ever since, but you're changing that— you have changed that." I look into his eyes, letting him see what I'm too afraid to say.

Nick says nothing, just lifts me and situates us up on the bed. He makes love to me slowly until I'm crying out as I come, moaning his name into his mouth.

A short time later while Nick sleeps peacefully beside me, I struggle to find it. I attempt to clear my mind and place my hands on my bump, close my eyes, and let my mind drift to the baby I'm growing and not everything else that wants to ruin our happiness.

NICK

I scan the jewelry case and spot the necklace I want to give to Sierra at the gender reveal party her sister is throwing us this coming Sunday. It's a diamond flower pendant in rose gold. "I'll take it," I tell the woman behind the counter.

She puts it in that familiar light blue box with a white ribbon. She sticks it in a bag then takes my credit card and rings me up. I hope Sierra loves it.

Sierra's at the studio, so I run home and stick the necklace in my safe. My phone rings and I pull it out of my suit coat. It's my sister. "Hey, Nadia."

"Hello, big brother. I got the invite to the party and will be there. God, I hope it's a girl. I'll make sure she's got the cutest little dresses." Her voice turns serious. "How is she doing?"

"Sierra is doing amazing and feels great. She's felt the baby move, but I haven't been able to yet." I know I'm pouting, but it's just not fair.

We talk for a few more minutes before we disconnect. Nadia did tell me before we hung up that my mom was planning on coming to the party as well. They've both begun treating Sierra better, but my father is still being a prick about it. Let's face it— he's a prick about everything.

I head toward the stadium to pick up the signed contracts on new vendors we're going to be using next season. This is definitely a learning experience, but I never knew it was going to be so time consuming.

Luckily I have an amazing team at each of my restaurants to run things while I deal with the shit that Gordo apparently doesn't want to, which I'm learning is just about everything.

The team is practicing right now and I watch them for a few minutes as they run some drills. I turn and head to the office. I find the signed contracts in a manila envelope and make sure everyone who was supposed to sign, did.

I stick them in the envelope and stuff them in my messenger bag. I'll file my copy away in my file cabinet at home. As I step outside I find a small group of the cheerleaders walking up to the entrance.

"Hey, Nick," a couple of them say as they walk by. I give them a chin lift and keep walking.

I'm almost to my car when I hear someone call my name. I turn to find Colton jogging toward me. "What's up, Colton?"

"Nothing much, but um… Could you do me a favor?" He holds up his hands in a surrendering motion. "It's nothing bad, but could you get Heidi's number for me? I know you know there's some history between us, but I want the chance to talk to her."

I'd rather deal with Staci right now than this. "Man, I don't want to get in the middle of this. If I have my way she'll be my sister-in-law in the future. Sierra would kick my ass if I gave it to you. Why don't you just stop by their studio?"

"I would, but I'm afraid it would cause a scene and backfire." He's quiet for a moment and then looks at me. "I promise I won't say anything, but I need to speak to her."

Everything inside me tells me to give it to him, but I need to think about it first. If this goes bad it could blow up in my face and cause problems for me and Sierra. I doubt the guy would risk his career for a chance to maybe make things right with Heidi.

"Let me think about it. I trust that whatever it is you have to say won't hurt her."

He's shaking his head. "Never."

I sigh. "Let me think about it, and I'll let you know."

The guy looks relieved, but I swear if this backfires and causes problems I will kick his ass. He turns around and jogs back inside. "Fuck me," I mutter as I climb in my car.

The rest of my day is spent putting out fires; a line cook got caught with blow, a delivery truck was late, and we had a computer glitch that erased all of our reservations at *Nicholas*.

Thankfully we were able to get an IT specialist out and they were able to retrieve it from cyberland. With everything under control, I make my way out to the parking lot. I pull my phone out as I climb in my car and see that it's dead.

I plug it in, and it powers back on. There are several missed calls from Sierra and text messages.

Sierra: Where are you? Are you coming? I'm here."

Sierra: The nurse just called me back. You better hurry.

Twenty minutes later there was another text.

Sierra: The ultrasound tech just came in. Where are you?

"Fucking shit! Dammit!" I pound on my steering wheel. I knew today was the day we were getting to see our baby, and I fucking missed it. I call her, and she answers on the second ring.

"You missed it." She's pissed, and I can't say I blame her. "Our baby is perfect, and they got a perfect profile picture. The baby gave the tech a perfect shot of whether they're a boy or girl."

"Baby, I'm so sorry. It's been one thing after another today, and I completely lost track of time. Where are you now?"

"At the studio. I have a client in an hour."

I pull out of the stadium parking lot. "Are you hungry? I could bring you lunch." It's not much, but at least it's something.

"Actually I grabbed something after the appointment. Just come by, and I'll show you the pictures."

We hang up. I stop by the florist and pick her up some pink roses, her favorite. Then I stop and get a dozen cupcakes for her and her sisters from a bakery that specializes in cupcakes.

When I have all the goodies, I make my way

toward Sugar and Spice, Ink. Traffic is crazy today, and it takes me almost forty-five minutes to get there. The lot is full when I pull in, but I'm not surprised.

The buzzing of the tattoo guns—nope, I've been yelled at for calling them that—the tattoo machines fills the space. Lainey, their apprentice, is sitting behind the desk. "Hey, Nick. She's in the office." I thank her and then wave to the other girls as I walk down the hall.

I find my baby mama sitting on the love seat holding a piece of paper in her hand. "Hey, babe." She smiles when she sees me, and relief rolls through me. "I bought you these. I'm so fucking sorry."

"It's fine, seriously." She pats the cushion next to her. "Come here."

Sitting next to her, she holds up a black and white photo. It takes a second to realize that I'm staring at our child, and I'm so in love with them already.

Sierra points at the photo. "He or she is giving us the wave. Now do you want to see something really cool?"

She grabs another photo and holds it up, and honestly I have no words. Our baby, with perfect pouty little lips, has their fist up by their cheek like they're posing. "This is incredible." I look at Sierra, and she's smiling widely. "We made a beautiful baby."

I grab her and pull her to me, kissing her thoroughly. "Ahem…" Pulling away from Sierra, I turn to find Mona standing in the doorway. "Don't mind me, but your appointment just showed up."

Standing, I help Sierra up and hug her. "Text me

when you're on your way home, and I'll start dinner. Let me take the pictures home. I promise I'll take really good care of them." I lean down and kiss her lips. "I'm really sorry that I missed the appointment."

Sierra cups my face in her hands. "Baby, you run three restaurants and co-own a football team. You were busy; I get it."

"No, I'm never too busy for you or our baby. I promise you this won't happen again."

"Okay. Will you take the roses home?" I like that she calls my place home. Hell, I can't remember the last time she slept at her place. Maybe it's time she officially moves in. "Thank you for the cupcakes. If they're any left, I'll bring them home, and I'll let you eat one off of me." My dick immediately gets hard at the thought of that very thing. She gives me a saucy wink.

"Ewww ... gross. Now I can't eat one," Mona says from behind me.

I smile at her. "I'm sorry, doll. It's all Sierra."

She shakes her head and disappears down the hall. I look down at Sierra. "I can't believe I forgot to ask. Did they see anything about the hematomas?"

"Everything looked good. The placenta is a little low, so they'll watch that, but as long as I'm not bleeding they're not too concerned." I must look worried because she wraps her arms around my waist and smiles up at me. "No, it's seriously okay. They would've told me if I needed to be worried. Now get the hell out of here because I have to work."

She kisses me and, with her roses in my hand, I lead her out to her workstation. I eye the guy sitting at her station. He's ripped and good looking, I guess, staring at Sierra as she walks toward him. The guy stands and hugs her.

Fuck, why do I have the desire to punch that fucker in the face? I know, because I don't want someone touching my girl.

Turning away, I head toward the exit. I find Heidi watching me, shaking her head and trying hard not to laugh. "Yeah, yeah, yeah," I say before heading outside.

Who knew that being in a relationship would turn me into a crazy person?

EVAN GRACE

EIGHTEEN

SIERRA

I slip my dress on, and it slides down my body stopping mid-thigh. My dress is soft pink with flowers all over it. The sleeves get wider as they go down my arms.

The weather is getting nicer, so I'm wearing a pair of brown suede ankle booties. I decided to wear my hair in a loose chignon at the base of my skull. My makeup is light with drops of an illuminator that gives my skin a dewy look.

Today is the day we find out the sex of our baby. I'm so excited I barely slept last night. Luckily Nick helped put me to sleep by wearing me out. I step into his bedroom and grab my perfume, dabbing some on my wrists and behind my ears.

I head out to the living room and find Nick sitting on the sofa. In his hands I see he's holding a robin's egg blue bag. "Wow, baby, you're smokin' hot. You look so fucking sexy with my baby in your belly."

I strike a pose before taking the hand he holds out to me and stands up. "You seem to be missing something."

I look down at my outfit. "I am?" Nick turns me around so my back is to him. "Nick, what's going on?"

"Today's a special day," he whispers against my ear.

I see his hands come around me and then a chain of some sort touching my neck. Nick leads me over to the mirror, and I gasp when I see the beautiful rose gold and diamond flower pendant hanging around my neck. "I-I don't know what to say. It's so beautiful." I smile at him as he looks at me in the mirror. "Thanks you so much."

Nick turns me in his arms and tips my head back as he strokes my cheek with his thumb. "I love you, Sierra, and I love this baby we made."

My eyes burn, and I blink rapidly. I must look like a fish as my mouth opens and closes, but no words come out.

He grabs my hand. "You don't have to say anything. That's not why I told you. I just really wanted you to know how I felt."

I push Nick down onto the sofa and hike my dress up to straddle his lap. "I do, you know. I'm just scared to say it." Leaning down, I press my lips to his.

Our kiss turns heated, and my ramped-up sex drive has me getting wet immediately. He reaches between my legs, into my panties, and groans against my lips. "Always so wet for me. Do you want to fuck, baby?"

My answer is reaching in between us and unbuckling Nick's belt, undoing his pants. I climb off of him and quickly pull off my panties while he pulls out his hard cock. As soon as I straddle him, I grab his dick, line him up, and sink down on him.

It's quick and it's dirty, but I love every second of Nick inside me. It takes no time at all before I come hard, and then I feel him bathe my insides with his cum as he groans against my neck.

Nick pulls his softening cock from me. "Go get cleaned up."

I lean down and kiss him before I stand and hustle into the bathroom to clean myself up, put new panties on, and touch up my makeup. Nick comes in, standing behind me. Tears threaten to spill down my cheeks as he reaches around me to touch the pendant.

It sits perfectly at the base of my throat. I place my hand over it and smile at Nick in the mirror. He leans down and places his lips against the skin behind my ear. "Let's go find out what we're having."

I'm filled with nervous energy as we make our way over to Joaquin and Mona's place. There are several cars in the driveway when we get there. The front is decorated in pink and blue flowers and balloons.

My sister opens the front door when we reach it. "Hey, you two."

I hug my sister and then Nick does before we head inside. My sisters, brother, Victoria, the kids, Lainey, and a couple of Nick's friends are here already. I show off my necklace to the girls while Nick greets the guys.

"Oh my God, Sierra, that's gorgeous," Greta

says and reaches out to touch it. "You're glowing."

"Thank you. I feel really great right now." The baby gives a little baby kick, and my sisters all reach out to touch my stomach, but the baby knows it and quits moving.

Mona shows me the food setup and the cupcake tower. "I made yours and Nick's favorite cake flavors and then just did a vanilla buttercream." I love almond flavored cake, and Nick's is just a simple marble.

"They look great. Thank you for hosting this."

Nick's mom and sister show up a short time later while everyone is munching on snacks. Nadia reaches me first and gives me a cheek touch and hug. His mom does the same.

I don't miss the way his mom eyes my sisters, but they roll with it. We don't care what others think. I'm surprised when I find out that Nadia follows Greta on Instagram and they stand off to the side talking—probably about makeup or skincare.

When it's time for the big reveal, Mona leads us all outside. "First off, I want to thank you all for celebrating with Sierra, Nick, and their families. I'm so excited for this next journey for you guys."

I hug Mona and then step back as Nick does. She hands us each these tubes with strings at the end.

"Are you ready?" Nick asks as he smiles down at me.

I nod. "Absolutely."

Mona counts to three, and then we pull our strings. Powder explodes into a pink cloud in front of us. Everyone cheers, and my man pulls me into his arms. "Fuck me. A little girl, and if she looks like her momma I'm gonna be in trouble."

We share a kiss that borders on indecent, but I don't care because I'm so freaking happy right now.

When we finally break apart, everyone congratulates us, and Iris declares that she's going to take her future baby cousin under her wing. I hug her tight and kiss the top of her blonde head.

Nick and I pose for pictures, and while I munch on a cupcake I post the pictures of us with a sign that Mona had ready to go that says "It's a girl" on my Instagram and Facebook, tagging him in both.

We say goodbye to the last of the guests before we take our leave. On the way back to Nick's, I can't help but let out a contented sigh. Today was perfect, and in a few months we're going to have a perfect little girl to love.

I grab onto the headboard as Nick gets behind me. He reaches around my front, strumming my clit until I'm panting. "Are you ready for me, baby?"

"Always," I whisper because it's the truth. He lines his cock up at my entrance and slams into me. My head flies back and hits his shoulder as he begins to move inside me.

Nick grips my hips so tightly I'm sure I'll have bruises, but I don't care. He loves me, and we're having a little girl. I'm on cloud nine as I thrust my hips back, meeting him move for move. "Fuck me, you feel so fucking good. So hot, tight, and wet."

He pulls out and gently flips me to my back. Nick grips my upper thigh, pulling it up and giving him better access to my pussy. He enters me effortlessly and begins thrusting inside me.

That familiar tightness begins in my belly and know I'm ready to come. He leans down. "Feed me your tit, baby."

I grab my breast and hold it up for him. He sucks the tip into his mouth, and I swear I come almost immediately. Now that my boobs are bigger and more sensitive, he can't stop touching them.

"Yes, baby, give it to me," he says against my heated skin.

Nick pulls back, holds onto the headboard, and begins fucking me hard. I cry out again as the desire to come hits me. This man can light me up like no one else has ever done. He plants himself to the root, and I feel it as he begins to come inside me.

He pulls out and grabs me, moving me around until we're lying face to face. God, he's handsome. "You take my breath away," I say quietly.

"I hope she looks like you," Nick says as he places his hand on my bump. Our daughter decides her daddy needs to feel her move, so she gives a little wiggle that he finally feels because he looks up at me with a blinding smile on his face.

I place my hand on top of his and kiss his chin. "Thank you again for my beautiful necklace."

"For you, anything."

It doesn't take long before I fall asleep.

NICK

Last week Sierra officially moved in. She sublet her apartment to Lainey and even left her the furniture. Now my girl is here to stay. I've set up a consultation with the decorator who did my apartment, to do the nursery. I told Sierra that she would have complete control.

It's been seven days since I've learned that I'm going to be the father to a little girl. I swear I've been handing out pink cigars to everyone I know. I'm on cloud nine, and I'm also terrified. She's going to be beautiful I know it, and I'm going to have to threaten any boy who gets near my baby.

My mother has already ordered the baby's christening gown, and we haven't even agreed to do one. Mona brought over some of Iris' baby clothes, and I can't believe we're going to have a little one who will fit into those tiny clothes.

Sure, I was around when Max was a baby, but I

guess I never paid much attention to how tiny he was. All I knew was my best friend was the most amazing father I've ever seen. I already told Joaquin that I want him to be our daughter's godfather.

My cell phone rings, pulling me from my thoughts; its Gordo. "What's up, Gordo?"

"Hey, man. I know you don't want to travel, but this next weekend is the game to win to put us that much closer to the playoffs, and it's against Colton's old team. I'd like you to be there with me as a show of solidarity. Plus, I thought we could talk to Mitchell, the owner of the Cavaliers, and see what we can do to get more people in the seats."

I sigh because I knew eventually I was going to have to go to an away game. "If I go I'm only staying one night."

"Okay. Let's plan to leave early Saturday and fly home Sunday."

I can handle being away from Sierra for twenty-four hours. "Great, I'll book the flights," I tell Gordo.

"No, we'll take my family's jet." He lets me know that he'll email me our itinerary.

I hang up and toss my phone into the passenger seat. I stop by Publix on my way home to get the stuff to make Sierra homemade chicken alfredo and her favorite dessert, crème brulee.

Sierra doesn't get home until nine-thirty, and my dick immediately gets hard when she walks through the door. She's wearing black leggings and a form-fitting hot pink long sleeved Sugar and Spice, Ink off-the-shoulder t-shirt.

"Damn, baby. You look so fucking sexy."

She comes toward me, and I smile because she's

wearing her necklace—she's barely taken it off since I gave it to her. Sierra places her hands on my chest, pushes up on her toes, and kisses me softly on the lips.

Her stomach growls, causing us to both laugh. "I better feed my baby"—I place my hand on her belly—"and baby."

We sit together at the kitchen island and eat our dinner. "This is so good, honey. Thank you." She reaches out and strokes my chin with her thumb. Sierra holds it up, and I see there is sauce on her finger.

I grab her wrist and bring her fingers to my mouth and suck the one with the sauce on it into my mouth. Sierra bites her lip, and her pupils dilate. I can see her nipple poking through the fabric of her shirt.

"You make me so crazy," I tell her. "I swear I'm constantly fighting getting hard when you're around."

Sierra stands so she's between my legs and leans in, kissing my lips. She pulls back and yawns loudly, covering her mouth with the back of her hand. "Sorry. I'm beat."

I knew I shouldn't have woken her up early this morning. I can also guarantee that she didn't take a nap either. "Go get ready for bed while I clean up. I have to work for a bit, but then I'll be in."

She nods before leaving me alone in the kitchen. I put the rest of the food into containers and place them in the fridge. At least she'll have lunch tomorrow. In my office, I turn on my laptop and look over the deposits for each of the restaurants.

In the morning I'll talk to Sierra about my overnight trip to New York. It's important that I go and show support for the team, especially with the playoffs within our grasp.

After shutting down my laptop, I shut down the apartment. This place is plenty big for us now, but this baby won't be our only kid, hopefully, and we could end up needing more room. Does she want a place like Joaquin and Mona's? I'll just add that to the stuff we need to talk about in the morning.

Once the news is over I head to our bedroom and find Sierra wrapped around the body pillow I brought her home yesterday. I jump in the shower quickly and then brush my teeth.

As soon as I slide into bed, I take the pillow from her and toss it on the other side. I want her wrapped around me. Her belly is starting to get in the way, but I love having it pressed against me.

I rest my hand there and feel a barely there bump. "Hey, baby girl. Your daddy loves you so much."

While I begin to fall asleep, I can't help but feel immense joy and love. I just wish that Sierra wasn't scared to tell me she feels the same.

I step into the bar and find my father sitting in front of the fireplace in a dark green wingback chair. He watches me approach, and of course he can't be bothered to stand. I reach down and give his hand a shake.

As soon as I sit, the waitress stops over to take my drink order. "Maker's Mark on the rocks please." She saunters away, for my benefit I'm sure. I don't miss my father openly checking her out.

It makes me ill, and to think the woman could easily be my daughter and some creepo dickwad could be staring at her the same way. I clear my throat, and he turns to me. He doesn't seem bothered at all that I just caught him gawking.

"Here, I had Frederick draw these up." He hands me a manila envelope. Frederick is a lawyer who's been a friend of my dad's for a long time. "Look them over and both of you sign them."

I pull the papers out and scan them, feeling my blood boil while I do. They're basically protecting my money in case Sierra and I split up. If we split up, she'll get monthly support and will have our child a majority of time. That's, of course, if the baby is mine.

"Seriously?" The waitress brings my drink before I dismiss her with a flick of my wrist. "You expect me to take this to Sierra and have her sign it?"

"You're worth a lot of money. You need to protect your assets."

I drink my whiskey and shoot daggers at my father, but he's oblivious. Fuck, he looks bored. "Sierra isn't after my money."

"That may be now, but money changes people. If she gets a taste of the good life, maybe there's nothing she won't do to keep it."

I swallow the rest of my bourbon down and signal for another. "If you'd try to get to know her, you'd see that she isn't that type of woman."

The waitress returns with my drink, and I thank her before sending her away again.

"If you want to amend anything just call

Frederick." He leans forward. "Nicholas, I'm not trying to be an asshole. Sierra seems fine, but there are too many snakes in the grass who want to trap a man like you. If she cares about you at all, she'll sign it. Hell, it protects her too."

We finish our drinks, and he settles the bill. He walks out with me, and we stop at my car.

"I'll think about showing her the papers," I tell him, but I have no plans of doing so. I don't want her to think that I don't trust her or that she'll go after my money.

"Call me when you get back from New York. I want to hear about your trip and meeting." I'm taken aback because up until now he's shown no interest in my career—unless he can get something out of it.

"I will. I'm looking forward to learning from him." He claps me on the shoulder and walks over to his BMW.

I climb into my Mercedes and toss the envelope onto the passenger seat. I head downtown to Sierra's studio. I just need to hug my girl right now.

On my way there I think about our conversation this morning. When I told her I was going to New York for an overnight trip. She was sweet and understanding. "I'll just stay with Mona and Joaquin. This place is so big and quiet without you in it."

I pulled her into my arms. "That's a good idea. I'd feel better with you there in case something happened."

"We'll be fine." She told me while patting her belly. I swear her belly is getting bigger every day, but she keeps getting more and more beautiful.

"What do you think about looking at houses? I

know I'm jumping the gun, and we technically skipped the dating part of our relationship, again, but I'm sure this isn't the only baby we're going to have, and we'll need the room."

Sierra's eyes widened. "You want to take that step?"

"Of course. What do you think we're doing here?" I haven't told her I love her again, but that's because I want her to say it first next time. If I have it my way we'll be married someday—no rush.

"If that's what you want then yes, I'd love to start looking at homes for us to raise our family."

I pulled her into a bear hug, or as much of one as I could. I told her I want her to start looking while I'm away in New York this weekend. I wanted to laugh when I gave her the price range because of the way her eyes widened. Yes, I like expensive things, but I'm smart with my money.

Now, I pull into the parking lot of Sugar and Spice, Ink. Inside, rock music is playing through the speakers and the buzzing of a tattoo machine accompanies it. Lainey and Greta are sitting at the front desk looking at the computer.

"Hey, ladies."

"Hey, Nick." Lainey smiles up at me. Greta answers the phone, so she just gives me a chin lift.

I look toward Sierra's station and find my girl working on someone's foot. She looks up and smiles when she sees me. Heidi is at her station working on a guy's back. I never did give Colton her number, but I have it saved in my phone. Maybe in New York I'll pull him aside and talk to him, see where he's at.

I'm not sure how long Sierra's going to be, so I

make small talk with Lainey in the meantime.

"Are you getting all settled?" I ask Lainey.

She smiles and nods. "Yes, thanks. Not having to worry about furniture was nice too."

"Good, I'm glad. Sierra's thankful I know, especially since she didn't have to worry about breaking her lease." Greta hangs up. "Sierra should be done pretty soon if you want to hang out."

"I just had drinks with the man who sired me and just need to hug my girl," I tell her.

Greta stands. She's the tallest of the girls and looks more like Miles: brown hair, brown eyes, and tall, lean bodies. I've never cared for piercings, well except for maybe ears, an occasional nipple, or even a nose ring, but on Greta they all just work.

She comes around. "How about a hug from me?"

I accept her hug and kiss the top of her head. "This helps, thanks. Tell me what's new in Greta's world?"

"Nada. Just poking holes in people and doing my Instagram thing."

She posted a picture wearing an Atlanta Fire jersey at one of our home games, and she had thousands of likes. We sold out of jerseys on our website. People love her, but I can see why; she's sweet, beautiful, and charismatic.

We shoot the shit a little while longer before Sierra finally finishes up and comes to me, wrapping her arms around my waist. "This is a nice surprise." She smiles up at me. "How was drinks with your dad?" I lead her to their office. "Uh oh, this must not be good."

"He was just his normal happy self," I say, my voice laced in sarcasm. I should tell her about the papers, but I don't want to upset her. Sierra sifts her fingers through my hair, and I close my eyes, enjoying the feeling of her fingers in my hair.

"I'm sorry, sweetheart. " I can hear the sincerity in her voice.

A thought occurs to me, and my stomach turns. I open my eyes and look down at her. "I don't want to be my father. All I want is for our daughter to know how much I love her and will love her no matter what."

Sierra smiles and cups my cheek in her hand. "That right there, what you just said, already tells me that our daughter is going to be one lucky little girl because her daddy already loves her so much. He'll do everything in his power to make sure she's happy."

"This is exactly what I needed. Thank you, baby." This woman has turned me into a mushy fuck, but I don't even care.

"You're welcome."

We make plans for me to take her to *Blaze* tonight when she's done, and I'm going to cook for her there. I'm looking forward to making her one of our signature dishes tonight, a filet with broccolini and parmesan truffle fries.

At the front door she kisses me and tells me she'll see me in a few hours. I climb into my car in a better mood than I was before.

EVAN GRACE

SIERRA

I rock my hips while bouncing up and down on Nick's cock. I moan as he reaches between us, rubbing my clit. I pinch my nipples and grind down on him, swiveling my hips as he hits deep inside me. My orgasm hits, and I throw my head back, crying out over and over.

Nick flips us and then puts me on all fours, coming up behind me and thrusting his cock inside me. He grabs my hips as he begins to pound into me at a punishing pace. "Fuck me, baby, you're so hot and so wet."

I fuck myself on his cock, and his headboard slams into the wall with each thrust. He plants himself to the root as he comes, and he groans as he blasts his cum deep inside. We both come down as he pulls his softening cock from me, and he kisses me before climbing out of bed.

He returns with a washcloth and cleans me up,

then he crawls in bed with me, pulling me into his arms. Nick kisses me softly on the lips before falling asleep.

Tonight I almost told him I loved him, but I chickened out. I swore I would never be vulnerable to another man again, but Nick's continuously proven to me that he's the right man to let in. I'm scared, though, because it's not only me now, but our daughter.

I still haven't told him about Staci and seeing her while I was out shopping or the bullshit she tried spewing to me. I just hope that keeping it to myself doesn't turn around and bite me in the ass.

From my perch on the bed I watch Nick place his clothes, shoes, and toiletries in his garment bag before zipping it up. He looks up from the bag. "I don't want to leave you." He's been moody since last night because he's heading to New York today for the Fire's game tonight.

"I promise you that I'll be fine, and the baby is fine. We'll be with Mona and Joaquin, so I won't be alone. This trip is important." I slide off the bed to stand in front of him. "We'll be here waiting for you when you come back. Maybe once you come home … tomorrow night we can start talking baby names."

His smile is bright and beaming. "That sounds like a plan, beautiful."

Nick's phone pings, and he pulls it out of his suit jacket. He looks at it and then up at me. "The driver's here." He grabs his garment bag, throwing the strap over his shoulder.

I stand and wrap my arms around his waist. Nick hugs me tightly to his chest with his free arm. "I'll miss you," I whisper. Shit, I really don't want him to go.

Nick places his lips on my forehead. "I'll miss you more." He places his hand on my belly, and our daughter gives him a swift baby kick. "Don't be mad at Daddy, baby girl." He raises his eyes and smiles.

I walk him to the door, and he kisses me one more time. This one turns heated, but all too soon he ends it. "I'll call or text you when I land, okay?"

I nod. "Okay. Have a great time, baby." I stand in the doorway and watch him walk toward the elevators, and he gives me a wave. I blow him a kiss as the doors slide shut.

Closing the door, I lock it behind me. I immediately miss him and roll my eyes at myself. It's not like we're together constantly, but knowing that he's going to be far away makes me bummed out.

I make myself some toast, and after inhaling it I head into the bedroom and crawl into bed. I bury my nose in Nick's pillow, inhaling his woodsy scent. "I'm pathetic," I whisper to no one in particular.

I get up and trudge my way into the bathroom and get into the shower. After I finish, I dry off and walk naked into the bedroom, grabbing a clean bra and pantie set. I moisturize and throw on my undergarments before I blow-dry my hair.

I wear it up in a knot on top of my head. My makeup is light, and I put a frosty pink lip gloss on my lips.

Donning my black long-sleeved Sugar and

Spice, Ink t-shirt, I throw on a pair of the skinny maternity jeans I bought. I'll admit I love the way they look on me. I slip on a pair of pink Chuck Taylors and then top it all off with my necklace.

I smile every time I put it on. Talk about a sweet and thoughtful gift. That's Nick though, always doing things like that. It's not always expensive jewelry, but sometimes just a meal that he would cook from scratch just for me.

I grab my overnight bag and pack the pajamas, clothes, and underwear I'll need. My makeup bag, hairdryer, and curling iron sit right on top. I zip it closed and carry it out to the foyer, setting it by the door.

After doing a walkthrough, I head out to my car and make my way over to Mona and Joaquin's. I'm going to ride with my sister to the studio, and she'll bring me back there when we're done.

I park off to the side when I pull into the driveway. As I grab my bag the front door opens and Iris, Max, and Fluffy come running out to greet me. "Hey, guys. How are you?"

"We're good, Auntie Sierra," Iris says as she wraps her arms around my waist, hugging me tight.

Max gives me a chin lift. "Hey, Auntie." He laughs when I wrap my arm around him, pulling him into my side. I give him a squeeze and a shake. Being a gentleman, he takes my bag and carries it into the house while Iris chases Fluffy inside.

Mona and Joaquin greet me as I step inside. "Thank you for letting me stay with you guys tonight. I'm just being a big ol' baby about staying alone."

My sister places her hand on my stomach, which

since it's really popped up I notice more and more that people are constantly touching it. "We're happy to have you. The spare room at the end of the hallway upstairs is all ready for you. We'll let you get settled, and then we can head to the studio."

I kiss my sister and hug Joaquin as I walk upstairs to find Iris sitting on the bed with Fluffy. "Aunt Sierra?"

"Yes, baby."

"Are you and Uncle Nick going to get married?" I freeze because he hasn't ever mentioned that, but it's not like I'm looking for a ring. If we ever do I want it to be because we love each other and not because I got pregnant.

I should probably keep it simple. "I don't know, sweetie. We haven't really talked about it."

"Okay." She hops off the bed, hugs me, and then bolts out of my room. I pull my stuff out of my bag and set it all on the dresser for now. I have a bathroom all to myself which is nice, so I take my makeup and hair stuff in there.

Yes, I know I'm only staying overnight, but a woman must always be prepared—plus, my sister is stingy with her hair products. I head downstairs and find Mona and Joaquin kissing in the kitchen. "Ahem..." I laugh when Mona turns toward me, her cheeks flushed. "Sorry to interrupt."

"No you're not." Mona says as she smacks me on the ass. "You've always been a cock blocker." She says that last part quietly, but Joaquin heard it because he chokes on whatever he's drinking.

He waves a hand, you know the universal signal that he's alright. "Sorry, Joaq," I say as I shrug my shoulders.

Once he composes himself, he smiles. "That's okay. You girls have a good day at work, and I'll see you tonight." He walks us out and kisses Mona before she climbs into her Range Rover. Yes, her wonderful boyfriend bought her a brand new white Range Rover because he wanted her, Iris, and Max safe whenever he wasn't with them.

I love that he's that way with them. I love that Iris and Mona have that, since Iris' biological dad ended up being a big pile of shit, and Mona didn't really date a whole lot after Sam.

"I'm so happy for you and Iris," I tell her quietly as we drive toward the studio.

Mona grabs my hand and gives it a squeeze. "I'm happy for you too, you know. Nick has proven himself to be an amazing man. He'll be a wonderful father to my little niece."

I squeeze her hand. "He is pretty fucking great."

On the way to the studio, Mona drives through Starbucks and grabs me a tea and lattes for her, our sisters, and Lainey. Before we're officially open for the day, we're going to have a little meeting about what to do when I have the baby because I'll be taking at least six weeks off.

We're also going to let Lainey start tattooing. She's been practicing on this fake skin we have and has done phenomenal so far. Greta has offered herself for Lainey's first tattoo on skin.

Once we're at the studio, I turn on the lights while Mona sets our drinks down and carries our bags back to the office. I let the girls in when they show up and then lock the front door.

"Hey, guys, I got coffees for everyone. I promise this meeting will be really quick."

We all sit, and Mona begins running the meeting. Our meetings are so informal and more like us just sitting around chatting, but the look on Lainey's face when we tell her she's officially getting her own station and is going to start tattooing brings tears to my eyes.

Mona wants her only doing small pieces for now, but still getting to put her art on people makes her day. Our goal is to have her doing small to medium size pieces by the time I take my maternity leave.

I head to the bathroom. I finish up and grab my phone out of my purse and stick it in the pocket of the cardigan I threw on. I want it close when Nick calls or texts me that he's arrived safely in New York.

My first client shows up thirty minutes later, and I get to work.

I stand and stretch my aching back. That's what usually happens when I'm bent over for any length of time. My second client of the day just left—satisfied with the work I did. I head to the office and grab a bottle of water.

Flopping down on the love seat I close my eyes just for a minute.

"Sierra?" I pop my eyes open to find Mona standing next to the love seat. "You were out."

I cover my mouth as I yawn. "Sorry, I didn't mean to fall asleep," I say, smiling up at her. "What's up?"

"You're next appointment just called, and she's going to be about twenty minutes late."

I try to space my clients far enough apart that it won't screw up anything if they're a little late. "No worries. Her design is pretty simple, and I doubt it'll take a real long time."

Mona smiles before leaving the room. I grab my water off of the coffee table and drink half of it down. I grab my toothpaste and travel toothbrush from my purse and quickly brush my teeth.

I'm heading back into the office when my phone rings. I see it's Nick, and he's Facetiming me.

"Hey, babe," I say by way of greeting.

He flashes me his signature smile. "I'm glad to see you. I miss you already."

Warmth spreads through me at his words. "I miss you too. How was the flight?"

"It was good, uneventful." He stands. "We're going to freshen up. Then we're going to meet Mitchell, the owner of the Cavs."

"Nick, come on," a feminine voice calls out, and that's when I find Staci coming toward Nick.

"Ummm … it sounds—ahem, it sounds like you have to go. I'll see you when you get home, I guess."

I disconnect as Nick's mouth opens. Powering down my phone, I shove it in my purse. My stomach turns, and the baby gives a little wiggle. Clearly she knows her momma is upset.

Why didn't he tell me she was going to be there? Was this all part of a plan for them to be there together? No, I'm not going there—Nick has showed me over and over he's nothing like my ex. It's obvious Staci wants my man, and she's desperate.

I take a few deep breaths and slowly make my way out front and try to ignore the sinking feeling in my gut.

NICK

When I get to the airfield, the driver stops in front of the sliding doors and then opens my door for me. He grabs my garment bag out of the trunk and hands it to me. "Have a good flight, Mr. Echols."

I shake his hand before handing him a tip. He thanks me before climbing inside and driving away. I head inside, and Gordo smiles as he approaches me. "Are you ready to have a good time?"

"I am. I'm excited to hear what Mitchell has to say." It hits me that Gordo looks nervous. "What's up?"

He looks behind him and then back at me. "Okay, I invited some other people to come with. You're not going to be happy."

I follow him to the sitting area and see Gwen and Holly, two of the cheerleaders for the Fire. They both wave to me. They're both nice, so that shouldn't be bad, but then Staci comes walking toward us.

"Hey, Nick. Fancy meeting you here." She winks before walking over to the other girls.

Leaning close to Gordo, I whisper harshly, "If this meeting wasn't important, I'd fucking leave. You're putting me in an uncomfortable position."

He starts to talk, but I walk right past him to sit in a single chair all by myself. I pull out my phone and shoot Joaquin a quick text.

Nick: Thanks for letting Sierra stay with you guys tonight.

A few minutes later my phone dings. I look, and it's Joaquin.

Joaquin: We're happy to have her. I take it your flight hasn't taken off yet?

Nick: Nope they're doing the final check before we can get going. I should be home by two tomorrow.

Joaquin: Do you need me to pick you up?

See, this is why he's my best friend. He'd do anything for me, and I'd do the same for him.

They tell us we can board, so I grab my bag and follow behind Gordo and the girls onto the plane. I grab a seat and stick my stuff in the seat next to me so Staci can't sit there.

Luckily she takes the hint and sits in the back with the other women. I stick my earbuds in and pull up one of the movies that Sierra downloaded for me, *Happy Death Day.*

She absolutely loves that movie, and it isn't long before I'm lost in the story.

When we finally land, I'm relieved. I want to call Sierra quickly and take a quick nap before getting ready for our dinner. Thankfully Gordo got us both a suite and the girls have their own room.

The girls come up to our suite and start having cocktails. I walk to the other side of the sitting room, grab my phone, and pull up the Facetime app, punching in Sierra's number. Once her beautiful face appears I feel happy and relaxed even though I already miss her like crazy.

"Nick, come on." I freeze because I know immediately that Sierra heard Staci's voice. She looks to the side, and she must see her because her face shuts down immediately.

I want to explain that it's not what she thinks, but she tells me she's letting me go and disconnects.

Closing my eyes I count to ten because I'm about to kick Gordo's ass and tell Staci whatever she's playing at she needs to fucking quit it. I try calling Sierra, but it goes right to voicemail. I ignore everyone and head into my bedroom, slamming the door and locking it.

I sit on the bed and scrub my face with my hands. Quickly stripping down to my boxer briefs, I climb into bed and take a snooze.

Mitchell stands as we approach. He holds out his hand, and I take it, giving it a firm shake. "Mitchell, it's great finally meeting you. This is Gordo, my partner."

Luckily, the girls are hanging back, letting us have our time to talk football. Plus, I'm glad for the brief reprieve from Staci's constant chatter. I swear she's trying to drive me insane, but I guess it's a good distraction from the fact that Sierra won't answer her phone.

On the way here I texted Mona and asked her to have Sierra call me. She responded almost immediately and said that Sierra was really busy, and she'd have her call when she was free.

I push the uneasy feeling in my gut away and focus on Mitchell. By the time our waiter brings the check, I'm in awe of this man. He's smart as hell and knows what he's doing. Besides owning the Cavaliers, he is a real estate mogul.

While we talk, I can tell he respects what I do and what I know. Gordo is quiet at first, but then he talks about our hopes for next season.

"You have the best quarterback we've ever had and I should be pissed, but Colton's backup is coming along nicely. Maybe we'll kick your asses."

I take a sip of my whiskey. "He's done a lot for us, exposure wise. He was a hometown golden boy who dropped off the map for a long time."

"It's not my story to share, but there was a reason. He's a good guy, and his teammates have a lot of respect for him."

I nod. "He's already proven that."

We head out, and his driver picks us up and takes us to the stadium. The girls follow behind us, and I can feel Staci's eyes on me, but I just ignore her. We head up to the owner's box and leave Gordo and the girls there, and I ask him to show me the vendors.

He and I walk around, and I talk to a few of the food vendors, asking what they find sell the best and their prices. Everyone is so welcoming and friendly. I even try samples of the stuff they sell.

We exchange business cards, and before we make it back to the box, Mitchell stops me. "Can I speak candidly to you for a minute?" Oh shit, what's he gonna say?

"Of course." What else am I going to say?

"If you are able to, buy Gordo out. No offense to him, but he doesn't seem to have what it takes—you do. I looked up your restaurants, and you've got the magic touch."

I nod, not saying anything because I'm sure what to say. I'm beginning to realize that maybe Gordo doesn't have what it takes to own a sports team, but honestly my restaurants are my life, and they'll always be my top priority.

Maybe after this season I'll need to reevaluate. Luckily, there's a clause in the contract that if after the first season I don't feel it's advantages are for me then he can buy me out. Of course, I don't even know if he'll have the money to buy me out if that's what I choose.

We head back to the owner's box just as the game starts.

I open my eyes and blink away the cobwebs. Warmth at my back has me freezing. I roll over and find Staci in bed with me, and she's naked. I jump out of bed, thankful to see that I have my flannel pants and boxer briefs still on.

She opens her eyes and smiles up at me. "Hey, you."

"Get the fuck out of my bed," I say with a shout. "You're fucking fired, Staci. This is the last fucking straw."

"Oh come on, Nick. Look at me. You can't deny that I'm a much better fit for you than that *tattoo artist*." She says that last part with a voice laced in sarcasm.

I would never hit a woman, but I'd love to throttle this bitch. "That tattoo artist is the love of my life and the mother of my unborn daughter. How fucking dare you try to sink your claws into me. Women like you are good for one thing and one thing only, and that's for some poor schmuck to stick their dick in, but that's not me."

"What's happening?" Gordo appears in the doorway.

I come toward him. "Did you let her in here?" I point to Staci who is getting dressed. "Is this fun and games for you?"

"Dude, she said she was just coming in to talk to you. I didn't think it would be a big deal."

"Get out! I'm getting dressed and going home." Thankfully they leave me alone, and I quickly get dressed and send for an Uber. I look up flights, and there is one that heads to Atlanta in three hours. The ticket is expensive, but I'll pay it. I'll fucking wait as long as I have to, but I'm out of here.

I brush my teeth and quickly pack up my toiletries. I grab my phone and try to call Sierra, but she sends me to voicemail. I leave her a quick message. "Baby, this trip was a bust, and I'm heading home. I'll tell you about it when I get there, but I think my days of co-owning this team are about over.

I love you."

My car is almost here, so I grab my bag and head out into the sitting area where Gordo, Staci, and the other girls are all sitting.

"I'm catching my own flight home. If you respect me at all you'll make sure that *she*"—I point to Staci—"is fucking off the team. I don't want to see her face again."

"Oh, Nick, relax. It's not like we did anything wrong." This fucking woman is something else. She is oblivious.

"You were naked in my motherfucking bed!" I roar. "I don't want you. I've never wanted you, but that doesn't seem to matter to you." Gordo comes toward me, and I hold up a hand. "Don't come near me because I will annihilate you."

I step out into the hall and take a deep breath. Once I'm downstairs and outside, I feel myself relax. I'll feel even better when I'm on the plane, heading home to my girls.

STENCIL: SUGAR AND SPICE, INK BOOK TWO

SIERRA

I decide to get out of bed because I can't sleep. Sitting on the side of the bed, I rub my belly as my daughter does little karate kicks. It's like she can feel my stress. I haven't been able to stop thinking about the fact that Staci is with Nick right now.

Before going downstairs, I use the bathroom, wash my hands, and then brush my teeth. I quickly put on a bra and throw my hair up in a ponytail on top of my head. The kids' doors are closed, and I'm sure they're still asleep.

Once I'm downstairs, I hear Mona's voice. "He's your best friend, but I'm going to kill his cheating ass." My stomach turns as I walk toward the kitchen.

"*Mi Amor,* we don't know anything for sure yet. Don't jump to conclusions."

They freeze when I come walking into the kitchen. "What's going on?" Shit, I don't even want to know.

Mona comes toward me. "Come, sit."

Joaquin pulls out a chair for me at the counter. He kisses the top of my head before disappearing out of the room.

Mona takes the chair next to me and turns to face me. "I was lying in bed this morning looking at my phone." She holds her phone out to me. "These were posted on Nick's Instagram."

I take her phone and look at it. The first picture is Nick, looking like he's sleeping. I swipe to the next picture, and my stomach turns violently. It's Staci lying in bed with him, snuggled close—it's quite clear she's naked.

I hand her phone back to her. "Can I move in with you guys for just a little bit?"

"You can stay as long as you need to." That comes from Joaquin who comes back into the kitchen and wraps his arm around Mona's shoulders.

I bite my lip to keep from crying. "Is it okay if I go back to bed?"

"Sure, sleep as long as you need to."

On autopilot, I walk upstairs and crawl into bed, pulling the covers over my head. For a long time I lay here praying for sleep to come, or to wake up from this nightmare.

I let Mona and me into Nick's place—it's no longer ours. She helps me pack up my clothes, shoes, and undergarments. After that stuff is all packed up, I head into the bathroom and grab my toiletries.

In the kitchen I leave my keys on the counter with a note.

Nick,

I came and got all my stuff. We'll figure out visitation once the baby comes. Thank you for reaffirming that I have terrible taste in men.

Sierra

Luckily it only takes one trip to get all my shit downstairs and into Mona's SUV. She tries talking to me on the way back to her house, but I just blindly stare out the passenger window.

Joaquin comes out to the SUV as we pull into the drive. "Go inside, cuñada, I'll bring your bags in." I love when he speaks Spanish. He's got names that he calls us all.

Joaquin's been teaching Iris Spanish at her request, and when they sit and speak it together it's so freaking cute. It's easy to see how much he's smitten with my niece and she with him.

Mona leads me inside and makes me go sit in the family room where the kids are watching something on TV. Fluffy gets up from his perch on Max's lap and runs toward me. I scoop him up in my arms and sit next to my nephew.

He may not officially be my nephew yet, but he will be; I know it. Everyone must sense my maudlin mood because they all just give me space, which I feel bad but appreciate it so much.

An hour later Joaquin looks at his phone and then shows it to Mona before getting up and leaving the room. It's probably Nick, and he's probably home now. I get up and head upstairs to climb into bed again.

I close my eyes tightly and pray that he doesn't show up. Thankfully, I'm emotionally exhausted and fall asleep quickly.

NICK

I step into my apartment and feel a weird

energy. "Sierra?" I call out, but I'm sure she's still at Mona and Joaq's. I should've gone there first, but I wanted to wash Staci's stank off of me.

Once I shower, I throw on some jeans and a t-shirt before heading into the kitchen to grab a bottle of water before leaving. Something on the counter catches my attention. Walking slowly over to the counter, I see it's a set of keys and a note. The minute I read it I grab my phone and try to call Sierra, but it goes to voicemail again.

With my phone held to my shoulder, I quickly dial Joaquin. "Nick." His voice is short and clipped.

"What's happening?" I look in the walk-in and find Sierra's clothes gone. How didn't I notice that before? "Where is she?"

"She's here, and you need to stay away. You know I love you, brother, but what you've done makes me question whether I know you at all." The anger in his voice is evident.

"Dude, I didn't know that Staci was coming. Sierra can't be pissed because of that."

He's silent for a minute, and then what he says rocks my world. "No, but she can be pissed that her boyfriend posted pictures on his Instagram of him in bed with another woman."

"What are you talking about? I haven't posted shit." That's when this morning and Staci in my bed comes back to me. "Hold on, there's been a big misunderstanding here. I went to bed last night alone," I stress. "I woke up, and Staci was in my bed. I didn't invite her, and I sure as hell didn't fuck her."

"Shit, man, check your Instagram."

I get on and immediately feel sick as I scan the

pictures. That crazy bitch got into my phone and took pictures with me while I was sleeping. I read some of the comments and get pissed.

Greta commented: You're such an asshole. You don't deserve my sister or my niece.

She ends it with a middle finger emoji and a poop one.

A lot of the comments are the same, but from different people. I save the pictures because I may need to press charges against her, but once I do that I delete the post.

I put my phone back to my ear. "That bitch must've got my phone open. I love Sierra and would never do that to her. I'm not that fucking guy. Fuck, I feel violated."

"Okay, I believe you. You need to get over here and talk to her. She's not in a good way, man. It's like she's shut down."

Fuck, I'm going to strangle that psycho. "I'll be there as fast as I can." I disconnect and slip on my tennis shoes. While I wait for the elevator, my phone rings. "Nadia, now is not a good time."

"Oh, I'm sorry were you fucking your side piece. Where's Sierra, does she know that you're a piece of shit? You know our father has hurt our mother before with his wondering eye. I thought you'd know better—be better than him." I don't miss the way her voice cracks.

The elevator door opens, and I'll lose her as soon as they shut with me inside, meaning I say what I have to really fast. "Nad, this has all been a fucking nightmare. I wouldn't do this to her, especially after what we grew up with. I have to go to her now, but

197

I'll talk to you later. I love you, okay?"

"Whatever." She disconnects. I'll have to fix that later.

When I'm finally in my car, I take a deep breath and try to calm my racing heart. The last thing I want to do is get into an accident on my way there. It feels like it takes forever, but the moment I get to Joaquin and Mona's my heart begins to race again.

"You've got some nerve coming here, you cheater." Mona comes stomping out of the house; obviously Joaq hasn't shared anything with her yet. "I'm going to make sure no one eats your freaking food or comes to your stupid g…" Joaquin comes out and puts his hand over her mouth. He whispers in her ear, and then she turns around and stomps into the house.

Joaquin comes to me. "You need to do something about that girl."

"I told Gordo I want her gone. I told her she was fired, but I have no fucking clue if I even have that power, or if we have to both agree. If he doesn't get rid of her I'm going to make him buy me out."

I follow him inside, and the house is weirdly silent. "Mona took the kids outside," Joaquin tells me before disappearing further into the house. I make my way upstairs to the bedroom that Sierra is staying in. I don't bother knocking; I just open the door and step inside.

STENCIL: SUGAR AND SPICE, INK BOOK TWO

TWENTY-THREE

SIERRA

I hear the door open but don't move. It's probably just my sister checking on me. It takes a second to realize that it's not her because I'd recognize his scent anywhere.

Throwing the blankets back, I sit up in the bed. Nick is standing just inside the bedroom, looking freaking gorgeous, and I just want to punch his fucking face. "Why are you here?"

Nick shuts the door behind him and moves farther into the room. "I know it looks bad, but I wouldn't cheat on you—ever. Gordo invited her to come, and it was him who let her into our suite. I woke up with her naked in my bed, but I swear to you that I never touched her." He scrubs a hand through his hair. "I have no clue how she got on my phone, but I did not post that shit."

"How do you expect me to believe you when at every turn she's there? The day I felt our daughter

200

move for the first time I overheard a woman talking to someone on her phone about the guy she was seeing and about him trying to break things off with his pregnant girlfriend. Lo and behold, I turn around and it's Staci."

I stand as he comes toward me, backing away so he can't touch me. "She told me that you thought I got pregnant on purpose, and that you were going to have me do the paternity test that your dad wanted. How did she know any of that, if you weren't involved with her in some way?"

My eyes begin burning, but I blink until the feeling passes.

"Dig deep, Sierra. You know that I wouldn't do this to you. As far as my father wanting the paternity test, maybe she heard me talking, but I don't give a fuck. That baby is mine, and you're mine."

Every fiber of my being tells me to believe what he's saying, but flashes of Lance flit through my brain as well as the pictures on Nick's Instagram. Maybe he didn't cheat, but he will because that's the type of men I choose.

I shake my head. "This baby is yours, but I'm not. I just don't think I can trust you." The words taste sour on my tongue.

"That's bullshit!" he roars. Nick stares up at the ceiling and then back at me. "You were just waiting and wanting something like this to happen so you could at least say that it wasn't you … again. Do you even love me because I love you? Saying it means something to me."

Is he right? Was I just setting him up to fail from the start? My mouth opens and closes, but the words are stuck in my mouth.

He looks at me closely and sighs. "I guess the next time we talk will be to discuss visitation because you're not going to keep me from my daughter." Then he hits me with the kill shot. "I thought you were the one, but I guess I was wrong."

The door slams shut after he walks out. Scalding tears flow down my cheeks. Our daughter moves inside of me, probably upset that her daddy just left. I back against the bed blindly, sitting as the room spins around me. "He really left," I whisper to no one.

Mona comes bursting into the room and rushes toward me, wrapping me in her arms as I begin to sob. Ugly, loud sobs wrack my body as I hold on tightly to my sister.

"Honey, what happened?" she asks quietly. "Joaquin told me that this girl set it all up."

I shake my head. "I-I can't talk about it right n-now. I'd like to be alone."

Mona kisses my forehead and then walks out of the room, shutting the door behind her. I lie down and curl up on my side and proceed to cry myself asleep because I just let the love of my life walk away.

MONA

As soon as I shut the door to Sierra's room, I feel the tears that were threatening to fall earlier slide down my cheeks. I've never seen her look so defeated before.

I quickly wipe the tears away, take a deep breath, and walk downstairs. The kids are outside with the dog, and Joaquin is in the kitchen making lunch. He takes one look at my face and pulls me into his arms.

"This is bad," I whisper.

"*Si, mi amor.* Let's just hope that they can work it out." I leave him to finish lunch and head outside to the kids. My heart is heavy as I watch them play together.

When Joaquin comes out and tells us lunch is done, the kids race toward the door. He stops me and pulls me into his arms. "We can't meddle because if they're meant to be together then they'll figure it out. I know this might be bringing up some bad memories for you, baby, but you can't get involved."

I nod. He's right because it does give me flashbacks of Sam, but I don't think Nick is going to ever walk away from his child no matter what—at least I hope that's the case.

SIERRA

I climb out of bed and feel like my body is full of lead. I go to the bathroom and then head back into my bedroom at my sister's place. Laying down I fall back to sleep almost immediately.

"Sierra, get up."

I blink away the sleep and stare up at my sister. "Go away, I'm sleeping." Rolling over, I pull the blankets over my head. The bitch pulls the blankets off of me. "Leave me alone. I'm tired, okay?"

Mona climbs onto the bed with me. "Honey, I know you're hurting, but it's not healthy for you to stay in bed like this. You've barely eaten, and you know it's not good for the baby." She brushes my hair back from my face. "I love you, but you're starting to stink."

I pull my pillow out from under my head and smack her in the head with it. "I guess I'll take a shower."

She gives me a satisfied smile. "Go do that, and I'll change your bedding, then we'll have some lunch." Mona shuts the door, leaving me alone. I grab my phone off of the nightstand and see that I have no missed calls. I know Mom, Greta, and Heidi have called Mona for updates, giving me the space I've wanted.

I haven't heard from Nick in over a week, but what did I expect—everything he said was true. I was just waiting for him to hurt me and to have a reason to push him away. The fact that I do love him and was just too scared to say it proves that I've got issues.

Shaking off my maudlin thoughts, I climb out of bed and reach my arms up above my head, stretching my sore, stiff muscles. In the bathroom, I look at myself in the mirror for the first time in a week and bite my lip to keep from screaming. My hair is a platinum blonde rat's nest.

Even though I've been sleeping a lot the purple under my eyes is a stark contrast against my pale skin. I brush my teeth first, and then brush them again, making sure I get all of the yuck out of my mouth.

In the shower, I scrub myself from head to toe two times and then shave my underarms and my legs. I stay under the spray, letting the water massage my sore muscles.

When I finally step out, I feel somewhat human.

I throw on a clean bra and panties. I get dressed in black knit shorts, a white tank top, and a red off the shoulder, long sleeve t-shirt with a white skull on the front.

My daughter gives a little kick. "I know, baby. Mommy will try to do better." I rub my hand over my belly that is starting to look like I swallowed a small basketball, but that makes me happy because that means she's growing.

Heading downstairs, I find Mona in the kitchen sitting at the counter with two plates. She smiles when she sees me. "Perfect timing. Come sit."

I take the seat next to her, and I look at my plate and laugh. There is a double decker peanut butter and jelly sandwich, a pile of cool ranch Doritos, and a huge glass of milk.

Growing up, our mom would make this for us kids when we had a bad day. We'd sit together and tell her our troubles while we munched on our food. My stomach growls loudly, so I take a huge bite.

I swallow it down, and it sits in my gut like lead. I take a sip of my milk and then turn to my sister. "What do you want to know?"

"What really happened with you and that guy in college? You changed after that."

She listens while I tell her everything that happened with Lance. I take another bite of my sandwich, but the bite feels just as heavy in my gut.

"Well, that explains why you haven't dated until Nick."

I shake my head. "We didn't really date. Even when he wanted to start dating we basically moved in together. Plus, there's this." I point to my belly, smiling as I grab Mona's hand and put it where my daughter is giving some kicks.

"That was my favorite part of being pregnant. I can't wait to do it again." Mona smiles at me.

My eyes widen. "Are you and Joaq talking about having babies together?" I sure hope so because they'd have very beautiful babies.

"Not anytime soon, but we both want more kids. Yes, we'd like to have them with each other."

I grab her and pull her into my arms, hugging her tight. "I'm so happy for you." I pull back. "What do I do? I love him, I do. I can't imagine going through this without him."

"Have you thought about contacting Lance and talking to him? Maybe getting some closure would help you heal and get past what *he* did and give you the courage to move forward."

I nod, and then choke down the rest of my sandwich.

STENCIL: SUGAR AND SPICE, INK BOOK TWO

NICK

This past week has been hell on earth. My sister and Sierra's no longer want to kill me. Of course I can thank Joaquin for that. He talked to Greta and Heidi and explained the situation, and they know that I love their sister, but if she can't get past her hang-ups there is no way we can have a future together.

Miles showed up at my place the day after I broke up with her and punched me in the face. I let him because I felt like an asshole breaking off things with Sierra, but I want her to come to me without that shield she's keeping around her heart.

On the business side of things, my lawyer is looking into what it will take for me to back out of the ownership of the Fire. Gordo is an asshole, and when I told him that I wanted Staci off of the team, he said I was blowing the whole thing out of proportion.

As far as I'm concerned, she crossed a line. Had a man done something like that to her, she'd probably had gone to the police and had them arrested. Staci tried to destroy my relationship with the mother of my child, the woman that I will love until my last dying breath.

I focus on the parking lot of Sierra's OB and wait for her to get here for her checkup. I want to go in, but I'm keeping my distance for now.

A few minutes later I see Mona's SUV pull into the parking lot, and I watch her park before hopping out. The passenger side door opens, and Sierra gets out. My stomach turns when I see her because she looks exhausted, and it looks like she's lost weight.

I send Mona a quick text asking for her to keep me updated after Sierra's appointment. Once they disappear inside, I pull out of my spot and head to *Urban Fusion*.

One of our prep cooks wants a shot at the sous chef position. He's been with us since culinary school, and I'll definitely give him a shot. He's going to cook for myself, the manager, and the executive chef. Plus, this will keep my mind off of things.

When I step inside, my phone dings, and it's a text notification from Mona.

Mona: The appointment went well. She's measuring a little bigger than her due date. The doctor doesn't like the weight loss, but she'll have her come back in two weeks to double check her.

Nick: Okay, thank you for letting me know.

The phone dings again, but my manager, Leah, meets me at the door. "Hey, Nick, how's it going?"

"It's good. How are Jane and the kids?" She started out at *Blaze* as a server, and I could sense greatness in her. Within a year she was the waitstaff supervisor, and a year after that my manager here moved away and I gave her the position immediately. She works hard for me and deserves every penny I pay her.

"They're great. The boys run us ragged, but I wouldn't want it any other way." We walk to the kitchen. "I hear you're having a baby girl. That's wonderful."

"Thank you. I'm excited." Most of my employees know what's going on in my personal life. I hated explaining that I didn't cheat on the mother of my baby. It's just another reason to hate that fucking cunt, Staci.

My father wanted me to file a lawsuit against Staci for defamation of character, but honestly I just want to forget that woman ever existed. I'll just be happy if my lawyer finds a stipulation to get me out of my contract.

Tommy comes out to greet me. "Mr. Echols, thank you for giving me the chance to cook for you."

"Of course. Everyone has to get their start somewhere." I clap him on the shoulder. "Dazzle us with your skills."

My executive chef, Sevrin, carries out waters for us and sits across the table from me and Leah. "What's up, boss?"

"Not much, man. I have a good feeling about the food we're going to eat today." Tommy has the fire and determination. "You know I have the gift for finding talent. Don't forget, I have the Midas touch."

"Yeah, yeah, yeah." I let him think he can give me shit, and really it's all in good fun. "You're the king, lord, and master."

"Don't you forget it."

We discuss our upcoming menu and decide on a day to come in so Sevrin and I can prepare the dishes for everyone to try.

Tommy comes out a few minutes later, followed by a couple of our kitchen staff who are carrying plates of food. He stops next to me. "Chefs and Leah, what I have prepared for you today is a grilled chili salmon with a lime crema on a bed of jasmine rice, topped with avocado."

I cut into my salmon and see it's cooked perfectly. I dig in and immediately moan. This has got to be one of the best salmon dishes I've ever had. "The crema keeps the chili from being too overpowering." I turn to Sevrin. "The rice is cooked well, and he got a nice crispy skin on the fish."

"It's definitely a summer entrée. We could even substitute the rice for maybe some grilled asparagus as well. This is all delicious, and I'd be happy to give him the opportunity to work with me. He's not ready to be a sous chef yet, but I'd be happy to train him to work with me"

"What? Do you mean some sort of apprenticeship?" He nods while he chews. "Okay, let me see how we could make that work."

Tommy comes out a few minutes later, and we talk to him about the dish and about possibly having him train with Sevrin. "Let me train you for six months and then you can cook for us again." My executive chef is an amazing guy who knows his shit. He's cocky, but he's got the clout to back it up.

I get up to take my leave a short time later and tell Sev that I just want to make some phone calls

EVAN GRACE

before we make any final decisions.

I'm almost to my car when I hear Sevrin call my name. I stop while he jogs toward me. "Is everything okay? You don't seem like yourself."

"Just some shit going on. Nothing I can't handle." Because I have no choice—I'm basically waiting for Sierra to decide our future, and I fucking hate it.

He nods. "Yeah, I heard you've been dealing with some shit. If you want to grab a drink and talk, just let me know."

He turns around and jogs into the restaurant. Pulling out of the parking lot, I turn toward my parents' place for lunch with my mother and sister. I'm sure they want to grill me about Sierra.

I pull into the driveway and park next to Nadia's BMW. I walk through the house and find them sitting on the patio under a big umbrella. My mom stands to greet me, and I wrap her in a hug and kiss her cheek. "Hello, Momma."

"Hi, my big, handsome boy."

Nadia tilts her head back for a kiss on the cheek. "Hello, big brother."

"Hello, baby sister." I take a seat at the head of the table and pour myself a glass of white wine as Gemma, my mother's right hand, places a salad in front of me. "Thank you, Gemma. This looks wonderful."

"Oh, thank you. Not as good as something you'd make, I'm sure."

"Don't be ridiculous." She squeezes my shoulder and then disappears into the house.

We begin to eat, and the salad is delicious.

"How's Sierra?" Nadia asks. "Have you stopped this boneheaded silent treatment?"

"I'm not a bonehead. She needs to realize that not every guy wants to hurt and deceive her, and until she does we can't be together."

"Mother, talk to him. This is stupid. She's having his baby."

My mom turns to me, grabbing my hand. "I don't know what happened to her before, but if it was bad enough to be scared, betrayal is hard to get over." She grabs my other hand. "Give her time, and if it's meant to be it will be."

"What's with the turnaround? You both weren't that nice to her."

Nadia lets out a harrumph. "You know what changed with us. Now will we be besties? No, but she's the mother of my niece, and she's crazy about you. I mean, come on—you're a pain in the ass. It takes a special woman to handle you."

I grab a crouton off of my salad and throw it at her. Before I leave, Mom brings me into her office. "I saw this adorable bassinet online and had to get it. I made your father put it together so you could see what it looks like. Isn't it gorgeous?"

I swipe my hand across the soft material. If I close my eyes, I can almost picture my daughter sleeping in this. "Where did you get this?"

"Crate and Barrel; isn't it just the cutest. It's so modern, and the top can be removed from the base and the baby can be wherever you are." She grabs several bags. "I've got onesies, sleepers, and a couple of little dresses, hair bows, and shoes."

"Wow, this is great." An idea comes to me. "I

need you to do something for me." I write down everything I want, and she tells me she'll take care of it.

I walk into the office, and Gordo is sitting behind the desk looking pissed. "I can't do this without you. You can't do this."

"Agree to fire Staci, and I'll consider staying." I take a seat across from him. "She could've ruined my reputation. She ruined my relationship with Sierra. I'm not going to explain myself to you again. You've got twenty-four hours to make your decision, but I should've never had to ask you to make the decision. You should've agreed to getting rid of her from the start."

Getting up, I walk out. I'm not fucking around anymore. I want this over and done with so I can move on.

On my way out to my car, I spot Staci getting out of her car. She sees me and freezes. For once she looks uncomfortable and unsure. She grabs her bag and practically bolts inside.

By the time I head home I'm exhausted, but that's what I do every day—I work until I'm exhausted, come home, shower, and then go to bed. I jump in the shower and then throw on basketball shorts when I'm dried off.

This time, instead of crawling into bed, I walk into the spare bedroom down the hall from mine. Right now it's got containers of clothes and other odds and ends in it, but I can easily empty it out.

That's what I begin doing.

Once I've got everything out of the room, I look around and imagine where the furniture will go. I can picture flowers stenciled on soft pink walls. No matter what happens, I want my daughter to have a beautiful space to sleep in.

If only her mommy can deal with what's blocking her so we can be together with nothing between us.

SIERRA

I step inside the coffee shop and look around. Lance lifts his hand and waves at me. I weave through the tables until I reach him. He stands as I approach, and we exchange an awkward hug.

"Wow. See, you look beautiful." He's the only person who ever called me that. Lance looks the same, but different. His skin is a golden tan, and his blond hair is short on the sides and longish and curly on top.

"It's good to see you."

I sit across from him. "When are you due? Do you know what you're having?"

Placing my hand on my belly, I smile. Whenever I touch my belly and feel my daughter kick, it brightens my day. "I'm due August fourteenth, and I'm having a little girl."

Lance grabs his phone and turns it in my direction. "This is our daughter Kelsey. She's two and a diva."

I take his phone and look at the picture. "She's beautiful."

The waitress interrupts us to take our drink order. He orders coffee, and I order an iced tea with lemon. As soon as she walks away, Lance turns to me. "I was surprised to hear from you, but I'm glad you reached out because there are a lot of things I want to say to you."

"I honestly wasn't sure if I even wanted to see you, but I'm at a crossroads right now. The father of this baby is the love of my life, and I couldn't fully give myself to him because I had a lot of trust issues after what happened between us." The waitress sets our drinks down and leaves. "I'm happy for you, I hope you know that. I can't imagine what it must've been like to hide who you really are, but you played with my emotions. I was just a pawn in the game you were playing. I loved you and thought you were the one. You slept with me all of the time and led me to believe you felt the same. Then you *never* apologized for it. You got your happily ever after, and I was left in the dust."

With the straw between my lips, I take a healthy drink. He reaches across the table, grabbing my hand. "I was a selfish asshole who should've been honest with you. I know I fucked up and did it in the worst possible way." Lance scrubs a hand through his hair. "So many times I wanted to reach out to you. I wanted to make things right, but what do you say to someone who you hurt like that?

"Chris was the one who kept pushing me to reach out to you. I should've done it when everything went down, but I was a chicken and ashamed. I really am sorry, sorrier than you'll ever know."

That is all I wanted to hear him say. I squeeze his hand. "Thank you."

Now that the heavy stuff is out of the way we switch to lighter topics. "Tell me about him," Lance says with a smile.

"Nick's amazing, and from the moment I found out I was pregnant, he's been so great. He loves me and would tell me all the time, even when I was too scared to say it back." I tell him about Staci and everything that's transpired because of her.

He leans back in his seat. "Wow. Sierra, I don't even know what to say. If you believe that he didn't cheat, then why aren't you with him right now?"

"That's the million dollar question. He's the first man that I've let myself love since you, and that scares me. No offense, but I love him more than I ever loved you. If you could destroy me, what could Nick do?"

Lance gets up and comes around to sit next to me. "I hate that I was too self-absorbed to see what my actions have done."

"I forgive you." He pulls me into his arms and hugs me tightly, causing my eyes to burn. Lance pulls away, and I can see his eyes are bright. "Now that the emotional stuff is out of the way, why don't *you* tell me what's been going on in your life. Tell me about your daughter."

We end up talking for over an hour. My heart breaks for Lance—when he came out to his folks, they quit speaking to him, but Chris's family accepted them both wholly.

Their daughter was carried by a surrogate, an egg donor, and a mixture of him and Chris' … stuff. They don't know which of them is her biological father, and they'll do the same thing next time.

When we're finished he walks me out to my car. We exchange phone numbers, and he wants me to keep in touch. Our daughters can make friends, he said.

I climb into my car and buckle my seatbelt. Lance stands next to his SUV and waits for me to back out before he climbs into the driver's seat. Smiling and feeling lighter than I have in a long time, I pull onto the road and head back to Mona and Joaquin's.

My stomach rolls as I stand in front of Nick's door, trying to summon the courage to knock. What if he's not alone? What if there's a woman in there? I lift my hand and knock quickly before I chicken out.

I wait and wait some more, but I don't think he's here. His car was in its spot, but that really doesn't mean anything. I reach up to knock again when the door opens, and there he is right in front of me. It's only been a couple of weeks, but I've missed him so much.

"What are you doing here?" His voice is flat, giving nothing away. "I'm surprised to see you since you have such terrible taste in men."

I wince at his words. Shame fills me because that's what I said in the note I left him. Taking a deep breath, I step toward him, but my heart drops because he backs away from me.

"I-I just wanted to tell you that I met Lance, my ex, for an iced tea, and he apologized for what happened between us. He actually had wanted to reach out for a while, but he didn't know what to say. Lance knew what he did was wrong, but he was scared to come out. His parents weren't accepting of his lifestyle, and that didn't excuse him letting me love him when I wasn't really what he wanted." I rest my hand on my belly. "I know I'm babbling, but I just wanted to tell you that ... that I love you, Nick. I'm so sorry that I pushed you away. You didn't deserve that. My hang-ups shouldn't have clouded my thinking the way that they did."

He doesn't say anything, just continues to stare at me. I ignore the sinking feeling coming over me. I back away from him. "I just wanted to tell you that I love you." I don't know what else to say. Turning, I walk quickly to the elevator. I want to be inside it when the tears begin to fall.

As soon as I reach it two arms wrap around me from behind. "You love me?" Nick whispers against my ear.

"I do. I love you so much." I begin to cry.

Nick turns me in his arms and kisses my lips as hot tears run down my cheeks. I feel us begin to move and then hear a door slam. "No tears, baby," he says as he brushes them away with his thumbs.

"B-but I hurt you."

"Yes, maybe, but I knew I just needed to give you time to get past what was keeping you from admitting that you loved me." Nick grabs my hand and pulls me through his apartment, stopping outside of one of his spare bedrooms. "I know we talked about looking for a home, but until we do our daughter will need a beautiful room to sleep in."

Nick opens the door and turns the light on. I step inside, and the tears begin to fall again, but these are happy tears. The walls are a soft pink with a baby animal mural on the wall. The crib is a light wood with pink bedding and a cream colored blanket draped over the side.

A matching dresser and changing table are against the wall across from the crib. On the dresser are a couple of pictures; the first is Nick and me Christmas night when we did our own gift exchange. We're both wearing Santa hats, smiling at the camera. The other is a picture of my sisters, my brother, Joaquin, Iris, Max, and Nick all posing outside of Mona and Joaquin's place.

The floors are beautiful wide plank laminate flooring that's covered in a plush looking area rug. A chaise lounge is in front of the wall of windows with a bookshelf topped with a pink lamp next to it.

Nick wraps his arms around me. "Do you think our daughter will love it?"

I nod because I can't speak. Instead, I turn in his arms, grab his face, and pull him down until our lips touch. I lean back enough that our lips are barely touching and smile. "I think she's going to love it."

Our kiss turns heated, and again we're moving and not stopping until the back of my legs hit his bed. With quick movements we divest each other of our clothing until we're both completely naked.

My belly has popped quite a bit in the two weeks we've been apart. I'm almost tempted to cover my body, but he looks down at me. "Fuck, you're even more gorgeous. Get on the bed."

He takes my hand as I climb on the bed. I scooch back until I'm resting against the pillows. Nick climbs on the bed, coming up between my legs. I've missed him so much I bite my lip to keep from crying again.

"Hey, no more tears, okay?" Nick comes up until we're eye to eye.

I reach up and brush his hair out of his eyes. "Okay."

Nick bends down to kiss me on the lips before his lips travel down my neck. I moan as he nips at the tender flesh at the base of my neck. He moves down to my overly sensitive breasts and sucks one tip into his mouth. "Oh god, that feels so good," I moan.

He releases it with a pop and then moves onto the other. Nick laves it with his tongue and then nips it with his teeth. All too soon he continues his descent down my body.

When he's finally down at my pussy, I can feel that I am soaked. At the first swipe of his tongue I cry out. "You are so sweet, baby." He begins to feast on me like a man starved.

My first orgasm comes out of nowhere, taking me by surprise. He fingers me into another one. When I come down, Nick flips me onto all fours, basically the only position that'll keep him from putting pressure on my belly.

He thrusts inside of me and my head flies back. "You feel so good—tight, hot, and wet." Nick's grip is hard on my hips, just the way I like as he pounds deep inside me.

"Help me get you there again, baby."

I reach between my legs and begin rubbing my clit. The beginning of my orgasm hits me like a shot. I cry out as he begins to pound in and out of me until he plants himself and comes deep inside me.

We both come down from our orgasms, and he kisses me between my shoulder blades. He pulls out of me and then gets out of bed. I lay on my side and watch him as he comes back in with a washcloth.

Nick quickly cleans me up and then crawls into bed with me. Our daughter gives a quick kick, and he smiles. She does a little wiggle inside of me. "I think she's happy we're back together," I tell him.

"Hi, baby, it's your daddy. I can't wait to finally hold you in my arms."

He holds me in his arms, and for the first time in weeks I feel good, at peace.

Nick kisses me on the lips. "I'm going to go lock up. I'll be right back." Before he climbs out of bed, he kisses my belly.

In no time he's back and wraps me in his arms. There is one question that I want answered. "Tell me about the trip to New York?"

He sighs. "I got to the airport that day, and as soon as I saw Staci, Gordo knew I was pissed. She was her normal aggressive self. At the game that night I hung out with the owner of the Cavs. He told me I should buy Gordo out because he didn't know what he was doing. Anyway, I went to bed early because I was beat—I woke up in the morning and found Staci naked in my bed. For a second I was worried she drugged me and had sex with me, but I was still in my underwear and pajama bottoms."

I lean in and kiss him right over his heart. "What happened after that?"

"I freaked the fuck out. I screamed at her and at Gordo and told him he'd better get rid of her."

"What did Gordo say?"

He grabs my hand and pulls it up to his mouth, kissing the back of it. "He acted like it was no big deal. I reminded him had it been a role reversal that I'd be in jail right now. I told him that if he doesn't get rid of her then he's going to have to come up with some cash because he's buying me out. Thankfully he let her go."

"I'm sorry. Wow, that chick has caused all sorts of problems. I'm sorry I didn't tell you about running into her that day at the mall. I never believed her." I look up at him. "I mean it. I know you'd never do that to me."

I watch the shadows dance across the wall and listen to his heart beating. "Have you thought about names?" It's time to talk about lighter, happier topics.

He hugs me. "No, I haven't. I guess it would depend on what last name she'll have."

"We could hyphenate her last name. You know Echols-Collins or Collins-Echols. Is that okay, or do you prefer just yours?"

Nick's quiet for a moment, and I'm worried I hurt his feeling. "I know we haven't talked about it, but don't you want to get married?"

"When we decide to get married, I don't want it to be because I'm having your baby. We'll do it when we know the time is right. "

He tips my head back and kisses my lips. "Welcome home, baby."

As I fall asleep in his arms, I do it smiling.

EVAN GRACE

NICK

The past two months have been crazy busy, but I've loved every second. My relationship with Sierra has grown so much stronger. Who knew that all her ex had to do was apologize to her and tell her he'd been a selfish asshole? That seemed to crumble the last of whatever was keeping her from fully allowing herself to love me.

Gordo got rid of Staci, but I think things between he and I are too strained, and he's looking for someone else to co-own with him. That's fine with me because as much as I've loved being a co-owner, it has taken up a lot more of my time than I anticipated. We made it to the second week of the playoffs before we were beaten.

I've run myself ragged the past couple of months, and that's not what I want to be doing when my daughter comes into this world. My father worked all of the time, and we never saw him—that's not what I want for my baby girl or Sierra.

We did our menu switch at *Blaze* and *Nicholas* last month, and they've been wildly successful so far. Sierra came to both menu tastings when I had the waitstaff come in and try all of the menu items.

Even pregnant with *my baby* she had several of the male staff eating out of her hand. That's just her, though. She draws people to her whether she tries or not.

Speaking of baby, I think we're ready. We've got a bouncy seat, a fancy ass swing, boxes and boxes of diapers, wipes, baby wash, and lotion. Mona brought us Iris' baby clothes and mixed with the stuff my mom and sister bought, this little girl will be stylish.

We decided to wait until after the baby comes to have a shower that way everyone could see and hold the baby.

My father has stopped pushing me for the paternity test, and together Sierra and I shredded the papers he had drawn up because I didn't want her ever thinking that I didn't believe that the child was mine. Every time we see my parents, she kills them with kindness, and someday she'll win the asshole over.

I focus on my laptop as I double check the liquor order for *Urban Fusion* before hitting send. "Hey, Leah, I just sent the liquor order," I tell her as she walks into the office.

"Thanks, Nick. How long are you taking off once the baby comes?" she asks as she sits in the chair in front of the desk.

I was adamant about at least taking the first

week off after our daughter is born. There is a lot of stuff I can do remotely, so that's what I plan to do. Hell, I may take another week if I feel like it. I'm not sure how I'm supposed to leave Sierra and our baby every day.

"A week for sure but maybe longer, and you know me—I'll have my phone and laptop on me, so I can work from home if necessary."

"You know we'll try not to bother you unless it can't be helped." That's why I have the staff I do. They are self-sufficient and are confident in their work. I trust each of their judgement.

My cell phone rings, and I see it's Sierra. "Hey, baby, what's up?"

"Nick, it's Mona. Don't freak out, but Sierra's water just broke. We're on our way to the hospital. Can you meet us there?"

I'm already out the door and climbing into my new cardinal red Mercedes Benz AMG G6 SUV. It was a sad day getting rid of my sports car, but time to get the Dad wagon. "Okay, I'm on my way. Is she okay?"

"Yeah, honey. The contractions are pretty strong already, but still about eight minutes apart."

My heart races as I make my way toward the hospital, but soon our daughter will be here, and that makes me so freaking happy.

"You're doing so good, baby." I hold a cold washcloth to Sierra's forehead. She's a warrior and has been pushing for the past half hour. Mona is on her other side holding her hand in hers.

By the time I got to the hospital, Sierra was already in her room and in a gown. Mona was sitting on the little sofa that was in front of the window. They started her IV and got her all hooked up on the monitor and then checked her. She was already dilated to a three.

Things after that have progressed rather rapidly. It only took five hours for us to be here with her pushing.

"Dad, look down and see your daughter's head." I look down and sure enough, there it is. "Sierra, give me another push," Dr. Honn says.

The nurse grabs Sierra's leg closest to me, pulling it back and then showing me how to grab it. Mona copies my hold, and Sierra bears down. I watch in complete awe as the head starts coming out.

"She's almost here." I place my lips against her sweaty forehead. "Keep going, babe, let's meet our daughter."

Dr. Honn tells her to stop pushing for a minute, suctions the baby's mouth, and the most beautiful sound fills the room. Our daughter begins to cry before her body is fully out of Sierra.

The doctor has her push two more times before our screaming daughter is on Sierra's chest. "Oh my god, she's so beautiful." She smiles up at me with tears running down her lips. I bend down, kissing Sierra's lips.

The nurse grabs our daughter. "We're going to clean her up real quick and then will bring her right back."

Mona kisses her sister's cheek. "I'm going to

call everyone."

She comes around the bed, and I pull her into my arms. "Thank you for being here."

"You're welcome, and congratulations, Daddy." Mona kisses my cheek before disappearing out of the room.

Once they have our daughter and Sierra all cleaned up, they bring our baby back to Sierra. The nurse helps get her situated in the bed, so we can get our girl latched on to Sierra's breast. It takes her a minute to get the hang of what's happening, and then she begins to suck.

"Our girl is a genius." Sierra smiles up at me.

I sit next to her hip and kiss her slowly and deeply before pulling away and returning her smile. "What are we going to call our little princess?"

Sierra tickles our girl's teeny tiny palm to get her to wrap her teeny tiny fingers around her momma's finger. I lean down, kissing the top of her head and inhaling her baby scent. "What about Ember?" I heard it somewhere before, and I just like the sound of it.

She doesn't say anything at first, and then Sierra whispers, "Ember Rose Echols."

"We can hyphenate her name. I'm very okay with it. It's not going to hurt my feelings; I promise."

Sierra shakes her head. "No, her name is perfect just how it is."

I kiss her one more time before standing. "I'm going to call my parents. I'll be right back."

"We'll be here waiting." I pull up my camera app and take a quick picture of my woman feeding our baby. "Hey, I must look scary as hell."

"Baby, you look more beautiful than anything I've ever seen. I love you so much."

She blows me a kiss before whispering, "I love you too."

As I'm walking down the hall, I spot Mona and Joaquin walking toward me. My brother grabs me in a bear hug. "I'm so happy for you," he says quietly.

"I hope I'm half the Dad that you are." I hold up my phone. "Go visit. I'm calling my folks, but I'll be right back."

They disappear down the hall, and I take the elevators downstairs. I swear I don't think my feet touch the ground as I head outside.

TWENTY-SEVEN

SIERRA

I walk down the hall to find Nick at the stove and our daughter in my mother's arms. My dad sits next to her, smiling down at his granddaughter. Nick is the first one to notice me. He smiles and then holds out his hand to me. "Did you have a good nap?" Nick kisses me.

"I did, thanks." I walk around to my parents, hugging my dad first, then kissing my mom's cheek. She reluctantly hands over my daughter who is officially two-weeks-old.

They just got here this morning and are spending the day with us before heading to Mona and Joaquin's. My baby shower is this coming weekend so, of course, they're here for that.

I rub my cheek against the top of Ember's head. Her hair is so soft, and it's already starting to lighten. My natural color is a darker blonde, and Nick's hair is a darkish blond too. I can't wait to see what she's going to look like.

I take her to the sofa and begin to nurse her. She's definitely a good eater. Now if only Ember was a better sleeper. If we're lucky she'll sleep two hours straight. Nick tries to stay up with me, but he's been going into the restaurants this week to check on things.

My sisters and brother have all come to spend time with their niece during the day, allowing me time to nap. I could never thank them enough. Nadia even surprised me and came to see her one day, and when I woke up she was doing a baby fashion show/photo shoot.

The pictures she took were amazing, and I asked her to have them printed out for me so I could frame them. I also told her that she should charge people because the pictures were great. Nadia laughed and acted like I was blowing smoke up her ass.

I focus on my little girl and pull her off one nipple to burp her before switching sides. My mom carries a plate into the sitting area and sits next to me. "Nick is such a good cook."

I nod. "He's amazing." She feeds me bites of the chicken salad he made.

Dad and Nick join us, and it cracks me up that my dad looks anywhere but at me. I grab the blanket to cover her, but my dad speaks up. "No, don't cover her up. I'll get used to it."

Once Ember is done eating, Mom takes her into the nursery to change her diaper. I finish eating and then go back for seconds. Breastfeeding has made me ravenous, and I'm constantly thirsty. Mona assured me that it was normal.

I head into the nursery to find my mom rocking her granddaughter in the rocking chair in the corner. I sit on the chaise lounge and return the smile my mom gives me.

"My babies make beautiful babies." She kisses Ember's head. "I really like Nick, and I love how much he loves my girls. Being blessed with five children, we wanted you all to have what your dad and I do.

"First Mona had the whole Sam mess, but Joaquin is amazing, and now she's so happy and has that adorable little boy as well. Your brother and Victoria are … whatever they are. If Heidi and Greta choose to find someone to share their lives with, I hope they're amazing as well."

Ember falls asleep, and I wrap her in the little contraption that keeps her swaddled. I lay her down and grab the baby monitor, and we join the men in the other room.

I sit next to Nick and smile as Iris holds her baby cousin in her arms. She talks to her in a sweet little voice and Ember watches her closely. Max held her for about two seconds before he was done with that.

I haven't been to many baby showers, but this one has been amazing. Mona and my sisters set up a big spread of appetizers and then ordered a bunch of pink cupcakes. The house is decorated in all pink, and Joaquin seems to be just going with the flow.

Speaking of Joaquin, earlier he was holding

Ember, and I swear Mona's uterus was begging for his swimmers. She probably spit out an egg or two with the way she was looking at him.

Come to think of it, after Nick took our daughter back they disappeared for a short time … hmm.

I grab my phone and take a picture of Iris and Ember and post it, tagging Mona and Joaquin in the picture.

The men load up our SUV with the gifts that everyone gave us. I'm excited to get her new clothes washed so she can start wearing them. Nick's mom got Ember a pink pair of baby UGGs; they're ridiculous but so cute. I can't wait for her to wear them this winter.

After the party, Nick calls ahead to the concierge at the apartment and asks for help getting everything upstairs. They tell him where to park and will meet us with a cart.

I stick Ember in her carrier and get her all buckled in. She's passed out and gives a sleepy little squeak. When Nick comes back in, we give everyone hugs and kisses goodbye. I thank my family for everything and thanks to my hormones I cry as we walk out.

Mom tells me they'll be over tomorrow to spend the day with us before they leave for the airport to head back to Arizona, where they've lived for the last three and a half years.

Once we get home, I get Ember upstairs while Nick deals with the gifts. He finds us in our bed, me lying on my side with our daughter sleeping soundly next to me. Nick climbs onto the bed, keeping our baby girl between us.

"Today was an amazing day," I say quietly.

He leans over Ember to kiss me. Nick settles back on the pillow and smiles down at the baby as he places his large hand on her belly. "Fuck, we made a beautiful baby."

"Don't say fuck in front of her. What'd I tell you? If her first words are fuck or tits, I'm gonna beat you," I whisper. I'm only half joking about beating him.

We lay in silence, watching her snooze, and I can't imagine my life without her in it. Nick gave me this precious gift, and I don't know how I'll ever be able to thank him or repay him for it. I guess I'll just have to love the hell out of him, which if I'm being honest, won't be hard to do.

I wake up and find myself in bed alone. I climb off the bed and head into the bathroom. Once I finish, I wash my hands then my face and brush my teeth. Staring at myself in the mirror, I'm surprised my body has bounced back the way it has. Mom said she was the same way, so I got her genetics, obviously.

My tattoos have luckily held up during my pregnancy. Just the ones on my hips got a little stretched. The elephant between my breasts is a little stretched, but it's a small price to pay for my sweet little girl.

Soon I'll be adding a pink baby rattle with Ember's name on it to my thigh. Each baby I have I'll add a rattle. I smile at the thought of having more babies with Nick. I would do it too. Kids never felt like a possibility, especially since I had planned on never being in a relationship again.

I pad quietly into the living room, finding my daughter in the arms of her father. Nick speaks quietly. "Having sex with your mom was the best decision I ever made." I shake my head, and he keeps talking. "I'm gonna work really hard to make her happy for the rest of our lives."

Stepping further into the room, he looks up at me and smiles that smile that can melt panties off in seconds. I come around and snuggle up next to him, bending down to kiss Ember's cheek. "I love you, and I love this family we've created."

"We love you too."

Right here on the sofa is the first, I'm sure, of many happy endings, and I can't wait to see how our story ends.

NICK
THREE YEARS LATER

I pull into the driveway, and the front door opens. Two little blondes followed by their beautiful mother come racing outside to me.

The past three years have been a whirlwind, and I've loved every second. Ember is three now, and she's sassy like her momma, but she looks like the female version of me; just like my sister. Our one and a half year old, Esme, looks like her momma, and hell, she's sassy just like her big sister.

Today we're finding out the sex of our new baby because I obviously can't stop knocking up my girl. Who can blame me? She's the sexiest pregnant woman. I love my girls, but I want a boy so damn bad I can taste it. My punishment for being a dog once upon a time is to be surrounded by beautiful women who I'm going to have to protect from all of the yucky boys.

"Daddy! You're home." Ember reaches me first

so I pick her up, hugging and kissing her before Esme hits my legs and hangs on like a spider monkey.

Sierra reaches me and wraps her arms around my waist, tilting her head back and waiting for a kiss. I'm always happy to oblige. I set Ember down before picking Esme up and smooching her. Once I'm done loving on my girls, I lead them inside.

"Nadia should be here soon," Sierra tells me.

I love that my sister loves her nieces the way she does. She spoils them and comes over to love on them any chance she gets. Nadia is happier than I've ever seen her. See, when Ember was a few weeks old she did a little photoshoot with her. My sister took Sierra's favorite pictures, printed them, and framed them.

Sierra loved them so much and got very emotional about it that she told Nadia that she should do it professionally. It took about a year of pestering before my sister took the leap. She's the only one who photographs the kids, but who better to keep them relaxed and having fun?

Now my sister is making some major cake taking pictures. She loves it, though, and she's this whole new person—not that I didn't love her before.

I should mention that after that first season I did have Gordo buy me out. Everything he did made me stressed out. Plus, after the Staci incident and his lack of support, I couldn't really stay.

We've seen Staci out a few times, but she's kept far away from me and my family.

My mother loves being a grandma, but she's never been hands on—not like Sierra's mom who immediately gets in the middle of our chaos. My father doesn't see the kids a whole lot, but I almost prefer it that way. He treats my children like they're causal acquaintances' children.

When Ember was six-months-old, we decided we were going to have more kids, so we found and bought our home. Every huge house we looked at Sierra said no. She didn't want some monstrosity. We compromised and bought a six bedroom, six bath modern farmhouse with an open concept.

We gave it a homey, modern, and clean look. Our kids needed to feel free to be kids while they were at home. Not worried about spilling or dropping something. Our pool is surrounded by a gate that is locked to keep the girls safe.

"Where are my favorite girls?" I hear Nadia call out and the click of her heels as she walks through the living room, dining room, and into the kitchen where the kids are sitting in their seats.

"Auntie NaNa." Ember couldn't say Nadia when she started talking, so it quickly became NaNa.

"Thank you for watching them." Sierra gives her a hug before Nadia comes to me. After a quick hug, I lead Sierra outside and get her settled into our SUV and make our way toward the OB's office.

"Hey, you two," Dr. Honn says as she comes into the exam room a half hour later. "How are you feeling, Sierra?"

Sierra smiles at me and then at her doctor. "I feel great. I'd like to say I have tons of energy, but with two kids under three that's not the case."

"Well, everything looks good. Your blood pressure is good, and your weight is staying on track. Let's have you lay back, and we'll measure you quickly." She pulls out the tape measure and quickly does her thing. "Okay, you're measuring just right for twenty weeks. I'll send the tech in, and then we'll schedule your glucose test."

She leaves, and I grab Sierra's hand, bringing it to my lips. "After we're done we'll go eat at *Urban Fusion*."

"That sounds yummy. I have two appointments this evening. Do you want me to bring either of the girls with me?" Sierra has cut way back on her hours at the studio, but it's not unusual for the kids to be there, usually sequestered to the office, but there is always someone watching them.

Their clients know that if they come to Sugar and Spice, Ink that it might be chaotic, but the quality is better than ever. Lainey is now an official member of the team, and they've brought on two other apprentices, which helps lighten the load. One of the sisters seems to always be pregnant, which makes things interesting.

"Leave them with me. You go do your thing, and we'll see you when you get home." I'm kissing her hand when the tech comes in.

Excitement fills me as the tech turns the light down and then squirts jelly on Sierra's belly. She places the wand on the jelly then moves it around as she turns the screen toward us.

"Here's your baby." She types away on the keyboard as she moves the wand around. "Everything is looking good. Did you want to know the sex?"

"Yes," I tell her. All I want is a healthy baby, but I really, really want a boy.

She smiles at us. "It looks like you have got

yourself a little girl."

I kiss Sierra's head. "Another little girl. She won't be dating until she's at least thirty, just like her sisters."

Three and a half months later our daughter Eva came screaming into the world, and two and half years after that I got my boy Emmett Nicholas Echols, and then I went and had a vasectomy.

SIERRA

I lie in bed and hear lots of giggles. I keep my eyes closed and pretend to be asleep as the door opens. "Girls, you have to be quiet until we're ready for the surprise."

"Okay, Daddy," our oldest, Ember, says.

"Daddy, I's have Momma's pwesent," our youngest girl, Eva, announces.

"That's good, baby. Ember, grab your brother and help him on the bed," Nick says quietly.

I feel movement, and then I feel tiny little fingers trying to peel my eyelids open. "Ma! Ma!" he screams in my face.

My eyes pop open, and I startle his little butt. I tickle his sides and kiss his cheek. Then I'm under a pile of babies. Nick stands at the end of the bed, smiling with a tray full of food, and Esme and Eva carry the gifts.

"Happy Mother's Day, Momma," they all say in unison.

My girls and my boy gather around me as I open

their gifts. The first is a diamond solitaire necklace. I smile up at Nick. "This is beautiful. Thank you."

The other package, I open it and gasp. It's a beautiful picture of all the kids. They're all in off white outfits, the girls have their hair up in buns, and Emmett is wearing a little fedora.

"You guys, this picture is amazing. Did Auntie NaNa take this picture?"

Ember snuggles up next to me. "Yep, Auntie Mona helped get us ready, and Auntie NaNa took the pictures. Do you love it?"

I kiss the top of her head. "I do, baby."

Nick places the tray on my nightstand. "Okay, monsters, let's let Momma eat her breakfast in peace." He bends down and kisses me. "Eat your breakfast and relax. The kids and I are gonna watch a movie.

He's always done this, whether it's my birthday, Valentine 's Day, or Mother's Day. Nick gets up with our babies and feeds them breakfast, and then they make a production out of bringing me presents and breakfast in bed.

These past six and a half years have been amazing. Yes, its chaotic and loud, but with four children I wouldn't expect anything less, and I love every second.

Nick and I got married right after Emmett was born. We planned to get married after Ember was born, and before we knew it I was pregnant with Esme. Time just kept passing, and we were happy the way we were.

I wrap my hand around the rose gold diamond heart pendant necklace from Tiffany he got for me

244

after our son was born. He's gotten me a new necklace from Tiffany's with the birth of each child.

I grab the tray and place it across my lap. He made fresh crepes and strawberries with fresh whipped cream on top. Esme was probably right there while her daddy cooked. Nick's already been teaching her, and the joy on his face every time she asks to help makes my heart melt.

My stomach growls, so I quickly scarf down my breakfast and take a drink of my coffee. I set the tray aside and take my coffee with me into the bathroom. I smile when I see that Nick's got my favorite bath salts sitting next to the tub.

There are also a dozen pink roses in a beautiful vase on my side of the counter. I draw myself a bath, strip out of my nightgown, and throw my hair up into a top knot. I sigh the moment I sink into the hot sandlewood-scented water.

I close my eyes the moment I lay back and just relax. The sun shines through the window, and I can feel the warmth on my face. The door opens, and then I feel fingers tipping my face up. "I brought you some fresh coffee. How were the crepes?"

"They were delicious; thank you."

"Take all the time that you need. I've got the kids handled." I feel his lips touch mine, barely. "Happy Mother's Day, baby."

I smile. "Thank you for making me their momma." He kisses me again, this time with lots of tongue. When the door closes again I smile because I'm the luckiest woman in the world.

Nick moves slowly in and out of me. I hold onto the headboard behind me as he grabs my thigh, using it to open me wider for him to bottom out inside me. I cry out and feel the tightening begin in my belly, signaling my approaching orgasm.

"You're going to come for me, aren't you?" He reaches between us and begins rubbing my clit in fast circles. "Let go, baby. Let me hear you."

"Oh god, Nick." I arch my neck and moan long and loud.

While I still come, he pulls out, flips me onto all fours, and begins to fuck me with punishing strokes. I flutter around him when he slaps my ass. He begins fucking me harder, reaching past me to grab onto the headboard.

I begin to come again as he plants himself to the root, coming deep inside me. Nick kisses me between my shoulder blades before pulling out of me. He goes to get a washcloth and then cleans me up.

Once that's done, we snuggle up in bed together. Nick's fingers trail up and down my arm as we lie there. "Thank you for an amazing day," I whisper against his chest.

"I should be thanking you," he says quietly.

I lift my head. "For what?"

"Thank you for giving me this amazing life."

What started out as sex turned into something I had told myself I didn't want, but oh how wrong I was.

EVAN GRACE

HEIDI

RELEASING WINTER/SPRING

I pin my hair up on top of my head and give it a quick spray. In my makeup bag, I pull out the illuminating powder and grab my contour brush. I add some to my forehead and above my cheek bones. I grab Greta's setting spray and quickly use it on my face.

"You look hot, girl," Greta says from behind me. She grabs my lipstick and quickly dabs it on my lips before stepping back. "There, perfection."

Out of the Collins kids, I'm the baby in the family. Greta is a year and a half older than me, but she's my best friend and my roommate. I turn back toward the mirror. "Are you sure?"

"Yes, you know I wouldn't tell you, you looked great unless I meant it. I went through your closet and found the perfect outfit." My sister is a fashionista and is really good at picking out clothes.

She disappears out of the bathroom, and I follow her into my bedroom. On my bed are my black low rider wide-leg tuxedo pants and a silver top that hugs my breasts, making them look bigger. Lord knows I could use all the help I can get.

Since I'm the youngest, the boobs were all taken up by the time I came along. I take off my robe and pull on some pink satin panties and a matching bra. I grab my perfume, spray some in front of me, and walk through it.

I slip my outfit on and slip on a pair of black stiletto sling backs. Looking in the mirror, I feel confident and sexy. My plan is to pick up some hot football player and have some much needed fun.

That's what I need, to have fun. Over the past couple of years I've spent most of my time building my clientele at the studio and proving to my sisters that I deserved my spot there.

I head into the living room and find Greta standing in front of the mirror, fiddling with her hair. I love my sister, but I can totally admit that I'm jealous of her. She's tall, lean, has gorgeous long brown hair, and is beautiful inside and out.

Her dress is a mixture of pinks, creams, and browns. It's a long, flowy maxi dress with long sleeves and a slit in the front. She's wearing brown thick-heeled sandals, which compliment her Boho chic style.

She smiles when she sees me. "Damn, I knew that outfit would look great. I ordered our Uber, so we should probably head downstairs."

We grab our purses, lock up, and head downstairs. Tonight is a party for Sierra's boyfriend Nick's arena football team. He invited us so we could hang with our sister, I'm sure.

When we reach *Blaze,* a man in an all-black suit opens the door for us and holds out his hand, helping each of us out. We step inside and head up a beautiful staircase to the space where the party is at.

We grab some champagne before searching out our family.

The party is in full swing, and there are hot guys everywhere. I haven't decided who I want to speak to yet. Nick calls someone named Colton over, and my stomach pitches, which is stupid because there are a lot of guys out there named Colton.

I turn toward Nick, and that's when my heart stops, and my stomach drops. Colton Winters is standing in front of me for the first time in five years. "Heidi." Just hearing my name on his lips has me turning and running down the stairs.

Outside, I run down the street with Colton calling my name, but all I can hear are the words he spoke to me five years ago. *"Heidi, I just don't love you anymore. This is over."*

Colton reaches me and stops in front of me, but I don't think—I just react, slapping him across the face. "Stay away from me," I grit out. "I just don't love you anymore." I throw those words back at him and flag down a cab, climbing inside before he can follow me.

It's not until I'm safely back in my apartment that I finally fall apart.

EVAN GRACE

STAY CONNECTED WITH

Facebook Author Page: http://bit.ly/2nGpUfQ
Facebook Reader Group: http://bit.ly/2osdDbR
Goodreads Author Page: http://bit.ly/2o07iYH
Twitter: http://bit.ly/2nGiBon
Instagram: http://bit.ly/2nusgxW
Amazon Author Page: http://amzn.to/2nulojT
Bookbub:
https://www.bookbub.com/profile/evangrace

Sign up for my newsletter and get the latest news
Newsletter Sign-up: http://bit.ly/2ncb8dv

EVAN GRACE

MEET

A Midwesterner and a readaholic most of her life until one day an idea came into Evan's head and a writing career was born. She's a sucker for happily ever afters and loves creating fictional worlds that others can get lost in. She loves putting her characters through the ringer, but loves when they get to that satisfying, swoony ending.

When the voices in her head give it a rest, which isn't often, she can always be found with her e-reader in her hand. Some of her favorites include, Aurora Rose Reynolds, (the queen) Kristen Ashley, Kaylee Ryan, Natasha Madison, and Harper Sloan. Evan finds a lot of her inspiration in music, movies, TV shows and life.

She's a wife to Jim and a mom to Ethan and (the real)Evan, a weightlifter, a home healthcare scheduler, and a full-time author. How does she do it? She'll never tell.

EVAN GRACE

ACKNOWLEDGMENTS

First and foremost, thank you to my husband Jim. Whenever I'm on a deadline, you always step in, handling the cooking and cleaning while I work. I don't know how I'll ever be able to repay you, but I'm sure I'll think of something.

To Lydia from HEA Book Tours, thanks for always helping me spread the word for my stories and getting ARCs into the hands of readers.

Kaylee, thank you for always answering my many questions and for just being an amazing person and author.

Diane, thanks for getting ARCs into the hot little hands of my ARC team and for keeping everything there organized and running efficiently.

Amanda, thank you for always being willing to read pages and helping me see things that sometimes I miss that first time around.

Evan's Entourage, my most excellent readers

group. Thank you from the bottom of my heart for your never ending support and enthusiasm, I love you all.

To Silla thank you for helping make my story the best it could be and for making it look pretty for my readers.

Ben my amazing cover designer, thank you for making me the most perfect and most beautiful cover ever. It was like you crawled in my head and knew exactly what I wanted.

**Check out these
OTHER TITLES
by Evan Grace**

EVAN GRACE

REALISM:

SUGAR AND SPICE, INK # 1

"A single parent, opposites attract romance that will captivate you from the very first page"- New York Times bestselling author, Kaylee Ryan

Ordinary, typical, conformed, are words never used to describe me. I've never been one to play by the rules. It's my world, my life and I do things my way.

I see the way they stare at my body covered in tattoos and my lavender hair, I just don't give a damn. There is only one thing in this world that can get me fired up, that's screwing with my daughter. As a single mom, it's my job to protect her, fight for her. She is and will always be my top priority.

So, when I get a call that she's in trouble at school, with a boy- no less, my claws are out and ready to strike. And the boy's father, some high society stockbroker, isn't about to deter me. I don't care how sexy, smart and rugged he is.

Opposites may attract, and I've been down that road before, it's one I never plan to travel again. A man like that would never be interested in a woman like me. That I know for certain, after all I'm a realist.

Chapter One
Mona

My alarm clock blares, causing me to groan. Those last couple tequila shots last night were such a mistake. Tequila has never been my friend, and I don't know why I thought last night would be any different. I push myself up into a sitting position, but that is a mistake because it feels like my brain is rattling around in my skull. I grab my head as I crawl out of bed and gingerly make my way into the bathroom.

After quickly relieving myself, I grab a bottle of Ibuprofen out of the medicine cabinet. I shake a couple into my hand, pop them into my mouth, and stick my mouth under the faucet. After swallowing them down, I shuffle back to my bed, crawl under the covers, and pray for death.

While buried under my blankets I feel my orange tabby, Peanut, jump on the bed, spin in circles, and then snuggle into my side. As soon as his furry ass begins to purr, I feel my eyes get heavy and let sleep pull me under.

I finally feel semi-human and climb out of bed, heading back into the bathroom. I brush my lavender-colored locks up into a bun on top of my head and jump into the shower. Once I'm scrubbed clean I feel more like myself.

Back in the bedroom, I throw on a pair of black leggings, white camisole, and a blue off-the-shoulder t-shirt. I pad through the house and stick a piece of bread in the toaster and brew some coffee. When the toast is done, I slather it in Nutella and then pour myself a cup of coffee.

Keys jingle, and the front door flies open. My reason for living comes running into the kitchen. "Mommy!"

I catch my daughter and lift her into my arms. "How's my beautiful girl? Were you good for Uncle Miles?"

My brother leans against the open doorway. "She was perfect as always. We had a blast, didn't we, Goober?"

"Yep, Uncle Miles bought me lots and lots of candy."

Of course, he did. My brother has been such an incredible help with Iris, but the man can't ever tell my daughter no. I set her on the ground. "Why don't you go put your dirty clothes in the hamper, and go play with Peanut because I know he missed you."

She kisses me and my brother before running out of the kitchen, yelling for our cat. I grab my brother a cup of coffee, and we sit at the little dinette in front of the window. "How was your girls' night?"

"It was good. Sierra was in rare form and forced me to do two shots of tequila after mass quantities of beer, and then I had to Uber it home."

There are four daughters and one son in our crazy family. I'm the oldest, then Sierra, Miles is in between us four girls, and then there are Greta and Heidi. We're super close, especially Miles and me. Maybe because he stepped in to be there when Iris' dad split, which was basically the moment the pregnancy test came back positive.

"I'm sure she had to twist your arm too." He stands and pulls me up into a hug. "I'm gonna take off. I've got a book to plot." Miles is a crime fiction writer and, the amazing man he is, a New York Times Bestselling author.

"Have fun with that, and thanks again for keeping Iris." I smile up at him.

"You know I'd do anything for my girls." He calls out goodbye to my daughter, and she comes running out to her uncle.

Iris launches herself into his arms. "Bye, Uncle Miles."

"I'll pick you up tomorrow from Kiddie college."

He leaves, and I smile down at my champagne blonde-haired, blue-eyed angel. "Today is a Mommy/Daughter day. We're going to make a veggie pizza, some chocolate chip cookies, and have couch snuggles."

"Yay! Can you polish my nails?"

I nod. "Of course."

She hops up and down. Her joy is infectious, and we start our Mommy/Daughter day, which indeed ends with snuggles on the couch.

At the end of our day, I tuck her into bed, brushing her hair out of her face. Iris gives me that smile that's like a balm to my soul. "Sleep well, baby girl."

"I love you," she whispers before rolling to her side and closes her eyes. I don't move right away; I sit and watch as she falls asleep. The steady rise and fall of her chest signals she's out.

From the moment she was born I've watched her sleep more times than I can count. She's the best thing I've ever done, and Iris makes me proud every day.

Is everything always rainbows and unicorns? No, definitely not, but my girl can handle anything thrown our way.

***

"What do you mean they want to have a meeting about Iris?" I look down at the paper that my brother brought to me after he picked up Iris from Kiddie College. He dropped her off at the tattoo studio I own with my sisters, just like he does every day.

Sierra and I started Sugar and Spice, Ink four years ago. We're all artistic and fell in love with tattoos and piercings. When I decided that I wanted to be a tattoo artist, I met with the one who did a lot of the ink on my body and got him to agree to mentor me. As his apprentice, I cleaned up the shop and answered phones all while learning to tattoo.

Sierra followed in my footsteps almost a year later.

Over the past four years, we've worked our asses off to make a name for ourselves. Because our studio is exclusively female artists, a lot of people didn't take us seriously. We had to work hard to get word of mouth referrals and prove we were just as talented.

We started getting followers on social media and really used the power of the web to make a name for ourselves. Now, four years later, we've been featured in Ink'd magazine twice, we've been interviewed on Atlanta's morning news, and we were even approached for a reality show, but declined.

I focus back on Miles. "I'm not sure, but they want you there tomorrow morning."

Miles and I step out of my office and head into the main part of the studio. I'm always in awe of the place we've created. The walls are a deep purple, almost an eggplant color, with white swirls. Our tables and chairs are black and chrome.

We have a lot of our artwork on the walls in frames. Some of the tattoos on display are ours, and Greta is on display for her piercings. My favorite photo is of the four of us girls in black Sugar and Spice Ink, sleeveless t-shirts, jean shorts, and red Converse. Heidi did our hair and makeup pin-up girl style.

We find my daughter and Sierra sitting in the waiting area drawing together. Through the entrance to the back, I hear the buzz of a tattoo machine, which is so fucking relaxing.

"Hey, sweet girl, why do they want me to come into the school and talk to them?"

She doesn't look up from her drawing. "I kissed Max," Iris says it so matter-of-factly that I'm taken aback.

"Who's Max?"

"Max Pena. He's my best friend." She has a smile on her lips. Man, I'm in trouble with this girl.

I sit next to her. "Did he not want you to kiss him, is that why I have to go in?"

She shakes her head. "No, he wanted me to," Iris says.

I don't have much longer to think about that because my last appointment of the day has just shown up. Since I have Iris, my sisters and I agreed it best if I open the shop daily, then I can get out of there by five or six, and I love them for it.

After my appointment, I clean up my workstation and find my girl in my office watching Tangled on my iPad. "Are you ready to head home, baby girl?"

"Yep."

I help her gather her stuff, and then hand in hand we head out to the work area and say our goodbyes.

Once we get home I make us some veggie quesadillas. Iris and I are vegetarians, which I wasn't until I was up in the middle of the night with a newborn and watched a documentary about where our meat comes from. After that, I just couldn't do it. I didn't set out to make Iris one too, but she loves to do what her mom does.

We eat at our little table in the kitchen, and she tells me about her day at Kiddie College. Things have been much easier this summer with Iris able to go there during the day.

After dinner, we snuggle on the couch and watch Modern Family. I can tell she's getting tired when she starts slowly tracing the tattoo of her name on my forearm. Sierra did it for me when Iris was a year old. *Iris* is done in beautiful calligraphy surrounded by gorgeous flowers.

Before she falls asleep, I maneuver her to the bathroom so she can go and then brush her teeth. In her bedroom, she changes into her pink nightgown with sugar skulls all over it.

Iris climbs onto her bed and under her purple butterfly-covered comforter. "Are you all snuggled in?"

"Yes, Mommy." I know my girl's tired. She only calls me Mommy when she's sleepy—much to my chagrin. "Will you lay with me?"

I crawl into bed with her and lean against the headboard. She rests her little blonde head in my lap. "Do you want me to tell you a story?"

She yawns and nods. "Tell me about the day I was born."

Iris has always preferred my stories over the ones in storybooks. I stroke my hand over her soft wavy locks. This is her favorite story, even though it was the easiest labor and delivery ever. "Okay, baby girl. It was two days before your due date, and I was working at a little tattoo studio by Georgia State." My mind goes back to that day...

My back aches, but I ignore it while I continue working on this arm piece. I've worked on this piece for four hours this go around and four hours a month ago. That time was just the outline and details. Today I'm doing the coloring.

I don't know why I keep working. My due date is fast approaching, and it's been so hard to work with my big, protruding belly, but I wanted to keep going as long as possible and to make as much money before his or her arrival.

I never expected to become a mother at twenty-two, especially a single one—no one does—but I'm ready and prepared. I'm just wiping off my client's tattoo. I let her stand and take a look at it in the mirror, smiling as she squeals with delight.

She comes back over, and I wipe some ointment on it before putting plastic wrap over it. I stand to walk her to the counter when I feel a trickle down my leg. "Oh shit."

Buck, the owner, is sitting behind the desk and looks up at my exclamation. The girl I just finished working on turns toward me as well. "Did you just pee your pants?" She laughs.

"No! Of course not, my water just broke." I turn to Buck. "Can you take care of her? I'm calling Sierra."

"You've got it, doll. Good luck."

By the time my sister comes to bring me to the hospital, my contractions are four minutes apart. On the way, I called my mom, and she's meeting us there.

Two hours later, I'm now dressed in only a sports bra and squatting in the water while leaning against the side of the pool, moaning through my contractions. I wanted a natural childbirth, and my midwife had told me about water birth, so that's what I decided I wanted to do.

My mom and Sierra help me through labor as my contractions grow stronger and extremely close together. As my stomach tightens, I rest my head on the side of the pool, moaning softly as my sister fans me, and my mom places a cool washcloth on my neck.

It isn't long before I'm hit with the desire to push. The midwife checks me and says it's time to start pushing. They have me squat in the water, and I begin to push. After pushing for a half hour, they have me reach down to feel the top of my baby's head. I moan as I push with all of my might, and then I feel the baby slip from my body.

They help me grab the baby, and as soon as they lift her out of the water, my beautiful baby starts to cry. The nurse lifts one of the legs and announces, "It's a girl." I begin to cry and hug my daughter to my chest.

Before my mom even cuts the cord, my daughter is latched onto my breast, nursing happily. I'd go through the pain of losing her dad and the pain of her birth to do it all over again.

"What are you going to name her?" Sierra whispers before kissing my cheek.

I've had a couple names picked out for both boys and girls and kept them to myself. I didn't want anyone to influence my decision. I stare at my beautiful baby girl and whisper, "Iris Clementine Collins."

Clementine was my mom's favorite aunt's name, and Iris because I've always loved it for a little girl's name, and it's my favorite flower. Both Aunt and Grandma lean in whispering their "hellos" to my beautiful baby girl.

"Mommy?"

I look down at Iris. "Yes, baby?"

"I love you." It warms my heart every time she tells me that. I can't imagine my life without her in it.

"Love you too." In seconds she's out, hugging her stuffed unicorn to her chest.

I slip out of her bed, turn on her nightlight, and shut the door. Out in the living room, I light my candles, turn out the lights, and grab my meditation pillow. I set everything up in front of the coffee table and ask my *Alexa* to turn on my *Chill Zone* mix.

On my pillow, I get into full lotus position, close my eyes, and clear my mind. I'm not sure how long I've meditated until I open my eyes and see that a half hour has passed. Peanut is sitting in front of me wearing the same bored expression he always does.

"What?"

He tips his head to the side and gives me a "meow". I reach out and scratch behind his ear and then yawn. His fluffy butt follows me as I lock the front door, check on Iris, and he follows me into the bathroom, watching me as I take care of business in here.

I strip down to my tank top and panties, curling up under the sheets and blanket. Peanut jumps on the bed, and I feel him circle his spot behind my knees before he settles in and begins to purr. Not long after, sleep pulls me under.

Chapter Two
Joaquin

I pull my Range Rover into the parking lot of Edgewood Community College where I've been summoned by Mr. G, the head of the kiddie college that my son Max attends. My son's a good kid, so I'm not sure why Mr. G wants to see me, and my son has said zilch.

I turn to my boy in the backseat. "You ready to go inside, *mijo*?"

My mini-me looks up from his tablet and smiles. "Yeah, Dad." He shuts it off and sets it on the seat. I hop out and meet him at the front. Max may be seven, but he's an old soul. I'm blessed to be his dad.

I'm a single father and have been since he was a toddler. His mother and I were never right for each other. She was the daughter of one of my father's associates. She was a gold-digging whore, and I wasn't going to let her lead me around by my dick.

She trapped me by getting pregnant on purpose, but she's definitely not mother material. Melina hired a nanny when Max was barely a week old. I, of course, fired the woman because I grew up with nannies, and that wasn't going to be the way my son grew up.

Max only sees her once or maybe twice a year, and it's usually awkward and confuses my boy. His mom's remarried now and someone else's problem—thank God. My cell phone rings as we walk through the halls toward the office of Mr. G. I look and see that it's my secretary, Lauren. "Hold up, Max. I have to take this." I swipe the screen. "Hey, Lauren."

"Sorry to bother you, Mr. Pena." I roll my eyes because I'm constantly telling her to call me Joaquin, but she refuses. "Your three o'clock appointment called and said that they could reschedule for four-thirty. Correct?"

"Yes, as long as they're my last appointment. I promised Max I'd grill burgers tonight, and I don't want to be at the office late." Max smiles up at me, and I ruffle his brown, shaggy hair. I'll need to make him an appointment for a haircut.

"You're all finished after that. I'll make the arrangements. Shall I have coffee waiting?" Lauren is by far the best secretary I've ever had.

"That would be great, thank you." I disconnect and shove my phone inside the pocket of my favorite dove gray Tom Ford two-piece suit. My shirt is a dark salmon pink color, as is the pocket square, and I'm not wearing a tie. On my feet are my favorite Ferragamo Benson burnished leather loafers.

We turn the corner, and I notice a woman with lavender hair braided and hanging over one shoulder. She looks up as we approach, and I'm hit by some unknown force right in the solar plexus. Her eyes are a sparkling cornflower blue. She's got lips made for kissing—*made for kissing?*

Her sun-kissed arms are covered in gorgeous, colorful tattoos. Her white t-shirt hangs off one dainty shoulder, black legging capris cover her legs, and hot pink Converses cover her feet.

"Iris!" Max runs past me to the beautiful little blonde who looks like her mom's twin, but without the lavender hair and ink.

"Max!" She jumps up, and they hug each other. They move to the opposite bench, talking quietly to each other.

"Um ... hi. I'm Mona." The lavender-haired beauty holds out her hand. I take her hand, ignoring how soft and small it feels in my much larger one.

"Mr. Pena and Ms. Collins, I'm Mr. G." I turn away from Mona and look at the short man with a major paunch and thinning hairline.

I don't miss the way he looks at Mona, what with the tattoos and the lavender colored hair; she doesn't look like a lot of the parents who bring their kids here. I hold my hand out, squeezing his hand a little harder than necessary. "I'm Joaquin, Max's dad."

"Pleasure," he says and then holds his hand out to Mona. "Please follow me into my office."

We both sit in front of his desk while the kids are led to one of the classrooms to give us some privacy. Mr. G sits behind his desk like he's all high and mighty.

The man looks between the two of us. "Before we begin, will Mrs. Pena be joining us?"

Had the moron read Max's information he'd see that she's not. "His mother is on vacation with her husband. He lives with me full-time."

The idiot nods. "Yesterday, there was a situation with your kids. It was snack time, and the children weren't with the class, so one of the aides went looking for them. She found the two of them by the bathroom, and they were kissing on the mouth." He crosses his arms and looks between us.

Before I can respond, Mona chimes in, "And???"

"Ms. Collins, we don't tolerate that sort of behavior here." The fat prick scowls at her.

Mona leans forward. "I understand that, but did either of them appear to be in distress?"

"Well no, but they're seven years old, and they shouldn't even know about that stuff." Mr. G stares at Mona with a judgmental look on his face.

Out of the corner of my eye, I see Mona tense, gripping the armrests of her chair. She looks ready to snap, and I do the only thing I can think of and put my hand on her knee. I don't miss the way she freezes, and I certainly don't miss the way she trembles under my hand.

I remove it and ignore the fact that it made my dick twitch and my pulse race a little. I open my mouth to speak, but Mona chimes in again. "They shouldn't know about that stuff? I beg your pardon, but people kiss in cartoons. My daughter sees her grandparents kiss. I'm not going to make her feel ashamed that she did it." She stands. "I will talk to her about sneaking off with her friends, and she won't do that again."

"Ms. Collins, I can see you're upset, but the kids aren't in trouble. We just wanted to make you aware of what happened, and maybe you both could discuss with them what is and isn't proper behavior in school." He stands from behind his desk. "I want you to know that your daughter is a joy to have in our creative writing class. She's got a natural gift."

We follow him into the classroom that's off his office and find Iris and Max sitting together coloring.

Mona sits across from them. "That's a great tree, Max."

My boy smiles up at her. "Your hair is pretty." He's a charmer, that's for sure.

Mona reaches across the table and grabs Max's arm. "Thank you. Iris, come give me a hug goodbye. Uncle Miles will pick you up and bring you to the studio, okay."

"Yes, Mom. I love you."

I walk around the table, ruffling Max's hair. "I'll be back after my meeting to get you. I love you, *mijo*."

As soon as I leave the classroom I spot Mona up ahead, but I don't rush to catch up with her; there's no point. Like I said, she's not my type. Plus, my focus needs to be on my son, not pussy.

I head downtown to my office. I have to prep before my meeting. My partners and I keep things flexible, which is great and I'm able to get off at a reasonable time so I can still be a father to my boy. My father is a workaholic, and growing up I watched as my mom grew to resent him.

They both began screwing around on each other, and that led to a nasty divorce. Now they live on opposite sides of the country. Dad is on marriage number four, and Mom is on marriage number two, but things are rocky.

When I divorced Max's mom I swore, I was never going to get married again. She reminded me exactly why I wanted to always stay single, but I'll never regret my boy. Once I reach the office, I park in the garage and head to the elevator, taking it up to my floor.

I share a floor with a marketing agency, but they're on one side, and I'm on the other. My partners and I have had our own brokerage firm for the past three years. Before that, I worked for my father's firm. When he decided to retire down in Florida, his partners became mine, and his clients followed me.

Our receptionist for the office greets me from his desk. "Good morning, Shane."

"Morning. I love that suit; it's my favorite," he says with his usual flourish. The man basically runs the office and is my personal shopper. He and Lauren are the backbone of the company. I'd be lost without either of them. He flirts with me a little, but it doesn't bother me; he's harmless.

I shake my head and head toward the back. Lauren stands as I approach. "How was the meeting?"

"My son and a little girl snuck off, and when they found them they were kissing on the lips. Iris is his best friend I guess. Anyway, the guy was a pompous ass. Iris' mom let him have it."

"My boys were rascals like that when they were his age. I'm sure it was harmless." Her boys are in their early twenties, and even though I'm thirty she treats me like one of her kids, but not in an obnoxious way. "I've got the conference room set up for your meeting. When they arrive, shall I bring you coffee?" She follows me into my office.

"That would be great." Lauren hands me my messages and then closes the door behind her, letting me get to work.

Free on Kindle Unlimited

Amazon US: https://amzn.to/2HR6zTU
Amazon Universal: https://mybook.to/RealismBuy
Add to Goodreads: https://bit.ly/2Crt6mb

AFTER WE MET

Gorgeous. Sweet. Funny. He made me feel things that I've never felt before. In just one short week over Spring Break, I began to fall in love. That is until it all fell apart. Now, here I am, three years later and I've moved on, at least that's what I told myself until he came crashing back into my life. Things have changed. I've changed, and there's something he doesn't know.

He wants me to give us another chance. I try to fight it, but it's not long before all of those same old feelings come rushing back. I know he feels it too. I can see it every time he looks at me. I can feel it every time he touches me.

It feels like I'm missing something though, like there's something that he's not telling me. Something that has the potential to tear it all apart. After all, it's not easy when you fall in love with your best friends' father. I didn't stand a chance after we met.

Chapter One
Lani

"Are you sure your dad is okay with me tagging along? I don't want to get in the way of your visit." My best friend, Molly, sits down next to my carry-on bag as I stuff my toiletries inside it.

She grabs my hand before I can zip the bag shut. "Of course he doesn't care. He said it'd be good if I brought someone just because he may have to run to the bar. Plus, he says that he's pretty boring and I'd want someone to go dancing with."

Molly's dad paid for my plane ticket, and when I refused to accept it, she made sure to let me know that her dad got non-refundable tickets. Molly told her dad that I'd refuse them—that's why he did it.

Of course he was taking a gamble that something would keep one or both of us from going.

"Okay, I am pretty excited to swim in the ocean."

I've never really been anywhere, and I've certainly never been to the coast. Growing up, it was just my mom and me. I never knew my dad, and my mom sometimes had to work two or three jobs to keep food on the table and clothes on my back.

I met Molly our freshman year at the U of I in Iowa City. We're both elementary education students. Now we're on spring break of our senior year. She and I are both so ready to be done and get teaching jobs. Part of the reason she wants me to go with her to Florida is that once we're both out in the real world, one or both of us could end up moving away.

My mom and I have had the discussion multiple times. We're super close, but she also knows that I'll need to go where the work is.

"Hello?" Molly waves her hand in front of my face. "Where'd you go?"

I shake my head. "Nowhere, just spaced out for a second. Are we taking an Uber to the airport?"

"Yeah, I figure that way we don't have to worry about parking." She reaches out, grabbing one of my sable locks. "Your hair grows so fast. I'm so jealous of your curls." She's one to talk. My gorgeous friend has sleek sheets of auburn hair, sparkling blue eyes, and a willowy body—with great breasts.

Me, on the other hand, I've got dark hair and eyes, light tan skin and I'm pretty muscular. I joined Crossfit after I gained my freshman thirty. Now I've got muscles and I'm fucking strong. Molly assures me all of the time that my body is still girly.

I grab my bag and Molly stands up. We're dressed almost exactly the same. We're both in black leggings, long sleeve t-shirts with zipped up hoodies over them. I'm wearing a beat-up old pair of Adidas and she's wearing Nikes.

She orders our Uber as I carry my bag and tote out into the living room and set them down next to Molly's stuff. Nervous anticipation fills me because I've never flown before, but I downloaded movies on my iPad to distract me and bought some books that I've downloaded on my Kindle.

When the driver is a couple of minutes away, we lock up and head downstairs.

It takes us about a half hour to get to the airport. After checking in and going through security, we

make our way to our gate. We sit next to each other—
I pull out my Kindle and she pulls out her phone.

Molly grabs her bottle of Xanax out of her purse
and breaks one in half and hands it to me. "This is a
low dose. It'll help take the edge off."

I take it, pop it in my mouth, and wash it down
with my bottle of water. My knee bounces up and
down while we wait to begin boarding. By the time
we're getting on the plane, I feel loosey-goosey. I
follow Molly to our seats, and I give her the window
seat because I don't think I'm ready for that yet.

When we're ready to take off, I ask Molly to tell
me more about her dad. I know that he and Molly's
mom weren't married for very long, and he owns his
own bar down in Key West. They had her young, and
unfortunately he moved away due to his job and she
didn't get to see him as often as she'd like.

Her dad's supposed to be the complete opposite
of her mom. Molly says he's a free spirit and a bit
wild, but a good and loving dad. I've seen pictures
and he's definitely hot. He looks like Samantha's
boyfriend from *Sex and the City*. I'm sure the women
hang all over him.

When we finally land, the sun is starting to set. I
look out Molly's window and am in awe of the view.
The water looks dark blue, and I can't wait to see it in
the sunshine. As soon as the seatbelt light goes off,
Molly pulls out her phone. "I'm texting Dad that
we're here."

I stand up and stretch my poor body—fuck me,
there's no room on these planes. Molly grabs our bags
out of the overhead compartment and hands me mine.

I follow closely behind her as we make our way out of the plane on to the tarmac.

Molly screams, drops her bag, and takes off toward baggage claim. I follow much more sedately and smile as she flings herself at—who I'm assuming is her dad. He sets Molly down and I smile as I watch him hug her tightly.

I hear her say my name, and then they turn toward me. My stomach does a little flip as he smiles at me. Oh God, I can feel my nipples hardening. What if he can tell?

"Lani, come meet my Dad. Dad, this is my bestie, Lani. This crazy man is my dad, Damon." Oh great, even his name is hot.

I reach my hand out. "It's so nice to meet you. Thank you for letting me come with Molly."

He grips my hand in his. I try not to stare at his beautiful face, but I can't help it. His square jaw is covered in light stubble. His blue eyes are highlighted by beautifully long eyelashes, and he's got lines around his eyes that just add to his gorgeousness. He's got that dimple in his chin, and full lips I want to kiss. *What?*

"I'm glad you could come and keep my girl company and you're very welcome." We follow him outside to his black Jeep Wrangler.

The wind blows through my hair as we make our way toward her dad's place. We pull up in front of the cutest little house I've ever seen. It's exactly what you'd expect a house to look like in a beach town. "You girls each have your own room with a Jack and Jill bathroom in between. Your bedrooms are upstairs. Mine is on the main floor."

We step into the house and I'm immediately in love. The floors are a light wood. The walls are a light tan-ish yellow with white trim. The sofa and two chairs are the color of watermelon.

I don't get to look too much before he shows us to our bedrooms upstairs. Full-size mattresses fill both rooms, but Molly's has pictures on the walls and nightstand. A teddy bear also sits on top of her bed. "I'll whip up something for dinner while you get settled."

"Thanks, Dad." Molly hugs him before he disappears downstairs. "Go get your stuff put away and get comfy. We'll rest until dinner is done."

On the way into my room, all I can think is that her dad is hot and it's going to be a long week.

Chapter Two
Damon

I head downstairs, ignoring the reaction I had to Lani. The moment I laid eyes on her, I felt like I'd been kicked in the gut. I've *never* in my forty-two years *ever* had that reaction to a woman like this before.

Wouldn't it just figure that she's forbidden times two: She's my daughter's best friend and I'm old enough to be her father. I grab the salad out of the refrigerator and the chicken breasts I've had marinating all day. It's a homemade marinade that Molly and I "invented" when she was visiting the summer after her freshman year in high school.

We named it Monroe's special sauce, I know… real original. It's got red wine vinegar, olive oil, soy sauce, garlic, oregano, and it's got a real nice tang to it. I take it out and turn on my gas grill. Once I place the chicken on the grill, I close the lid and run the bowl inside.

I head back outside and take a drink of my beer when arms wrap around my waist. I wrap my arm around Molly's shoulders and hug her into my side, kissing her forehead. This beautiful girl is the best thing I've ever done. I tried making it work with her mom, but she was jealous and never trusted me.

Every time I had to travel and do a shoot, she'd accuse me of cheating, which I never did. It got to be too much, so when Molly was three, we split. At first, I was able to see her a lot, but when the modeling jobs started drying up, I got offered a job and worked for a short time at one of the TV stations here, but I hated it.

I decided to buy an old run-down bar that was no longer open. It took me almost a year to get it to where I wanted it and now *Molly's* is a hot spot. We're right near the water, which makes it a tourist attraction. We're nothing special, no gimmicks, no dance floor, but we still pack them in.

"Oh, is that Monroe's special sauce?" She takes a big whiff and I swear I hear her stomach growl.

"Of course it is. I bought a couple bottles of Riesling for you. I know you said that you liked sweet wines. Tomorrow night I'm throwing you girls a welcoming party. It's nothing big just a few friends that want to see you, and meet Lani."

She gives me another squeeze. "That's great. I've missed you," Molly says quietly. She's always been a daddy's girl even when we were far apart.

"I've missed you too, baby." Out of the corner of my eye, I find Lani standing a few feet away from us looking unsure of herself. "Lani, I hope you like chicken."

She walks toward us. "I do, thanks. Your home is really beautiful, Mr. Monroe."

"Nope, don't call me mister, it makes me feel old." The lights above the grill show off the pink tinge of her cheeks. "Please just call me Damon." I look to my daughter. "Why don't you ladies get a drink and set the table by the pool. Dinner will be ready in about five minutes."

Molly grabs Lani's arm and drags her toward the house. My eyes immediately go to Lani's ass in the little shorts she's wearing. Fuck, her legs go on and on, and… of course she turns and catches me staring at her.

Free on Kindle Unlimited

Amazon: mybook.to/AfterWeMet

Add to your Goodreads TBR:
https://www.goodreads.com/book/show/46130978-after-we-met

Made in the USA
Las Vegas, NV
12 September 2021

OUR ARRANGEMENT WAS SIMPLE—
JUST PHYSICAL AND DEFINITELY NO
FALLING IN LOVE.

That seemed easy enough
until a positive pregnancy test changed everything.
He's loud, crude, sexy, and can cook
and he's bound and determined to make me his,
but I've been burned before and if I let him in,
and things don't work out for us, well,
it's more than just my heart on the line.

Can I push past my issues to open my heart
to that big beautiful man?
As we navigate this unfamiliar terrain
his enthusiasm begins to knock down the walls
I've always kept around me, but we keep hitting obstacles
that could ruin everything we're trying to build.

AM I STRONG ENOUGH TO BATTLE MY OWN DEMONS
TO MOVE FORWARD TO A FUTURE
THAT COULD PROMISE TO BE
EVERYTHING I COULD'VE HOPED FOR?

SUGAR
&SPICE
INK

www.authorevangrace.com

ISBN 9781696711302

90000

9 781696 711302

SAMUEL C. WILLIAMSON

Is Sunday School Destroying Our Kids?

How Moralism Suffocates Grace